The Kingdom of Nowt

by

Richard Stone

authorHOUSE™

1663 LIBERTY DRIVE, SUITE 200
BLOOMINGTON, INDIANA 47403
(800) 839-8640
WWW.AUTHORHOUSE.COM

First published by AuthorHouse 08/25/05

ISBN: 1-4208-7413-6 (sc)

Printed in the United States of America
Bloomington, Indiana

This book is printed on acid-free paper.

Chapter 1

The night was especially gloomy. Rain pounded on the roof so hard that it echoed like continuous thunder throughout the house. All the while seven-year old Ben Jameson slept deep within the covers surrounded by huge pillows. Thurston, Ben's long-haired tabby cat, was curled into a ball beside his head.

When the rain stopped, the light of the moon tore through the clouds and shot like an arrow into his room, flashing across his face. Ben slowly opened his eyes. Without moving, he surveyed the room. First left. Then right. Amid the slow, sweeping sway of the wind he heard strange voices and music outside! He shut his eyes tight. This is a dream, he thought, but the sounds from outside continued to float in, filling his ears and mingling with the soft thud of his fearful heart.

He opened his eyes again. Thurston sat up and stared at the window. Suddenly, the cat hissed and growled, then ran from the room through the crack in the door.

Ben's whole body froze. His heart pounded louder in his ears as the unfamiliar sounds echoed outside. What are they saying? he wondered. Is that my name they're calling?

"Ben, Ben, Ben," came the low, rumbling chant.

It is me! he thought.

"Ben be gotten, Ben be good. Ben, who shook the tree, so strong, so free. Ben, it's you we call, to play and sing. It's you, the heart of the kingdom's ring. Come down now from your lofty room. Meet your brethren of the moon. Wriggle from those covers. Open that mouth. No more must it be frozen with fear and doubt. Come down and meet your friends of Nowt. We have chosen you to speak. To fight all those who would kill, plunder, and cheat."

As Ben lay there he wondered who was calling themselves "his friends?" Where or what is a Nowt? What did they mean, "We have chosen you to speak, to fight all those who would kill, plunder, and cheat?"

The songs continued to float into the room. Curious, Ben swung his feet from the bed to the floor and crept to the window's edge. It was no more than five paces, but right then it seemed to stretch as far as the big field at Grandpa's house. Step. Step. Step. Step. Step.

When he reached the window, he closed his eyes, rubbed them, then opened them again. What he saw was so odd that he turned and looked back to be certain that he was in his own room. He looked out again. Tears rolled down his cheeks and splashed to the floor. He didn't know why. The feelings that filled his heart were unlike any he had ever felt before. Yet he began smiling, and laughing. And his toes started wiggling and flapping. Because there before him were trees sprouting from the heads of mighty giants that walked about! They were creatures bigger than dinosaurs, with trunks and bushes growing from the tufts of dirt on top of their heads. Swaying and flowing and dancing with mirth, some of the creatures blew into the hollows of their arms, making the most beautiful sounds. Others tapped their fingers against their trunks—bam dee dee bam bam boom bom bom. It was like a parade. Who would believe this sight? Bushes strung from the frowns of big fellows bellowing huge sounds, "Sing ho ho, sing ho ho, ah yee nah sen hah yah ho!"

Some creatures had palm trees sprouting from their noses like long snouts. The cutest of all were the teeny fellas no more than six inches tall with flowers of a thousand different colors growing from their straw hats. Then there were the stocky guys, arm in arm, with green shrubs growing from their shoulders, big and strong.

His favorite though were the little purple ones, marching with long grasses growing from their hips. Every few steps they'd tumble and fall. On their heels strutted little moon-shaped creatures with red, ripe tomatoes swinging from their hair.

They came in all shapes, sizes, and colors. Sweetgums, ginkgos, willows, and pecans. Pin oaks, hickories, magnolias, and fruit trees with pears and apples hanging from round bald spots on their crown. Birch, dogwood, orange, and tupelos with the furriest eyebrows. Poplars, basswoods, pines, and spruce, marching in step.

The flower creatures followed close behind. Arrowhead, butter-and-eggs, monkeyflowers, and morning glories. Lillies, columbines, skunk cabbage, and squawroot. Paintbrush, bluebells, nightshade, and bright red roses. Together they sang in perfect harmony, "Ohhh yahhh hohhh, yeee sahhh tohhh, yeee rahhh yohhh, lahhh teee dohhhhhhh."

These were the plants and trees that lived in his garden and in the woods behind his house. But there were some he had never seen before. As they gathered round under his bedroom window, they started to make funny sounds. "Iggly wok an boo don doo. Lis doo doo, she bar a hoo."

Are these words? Ben wondered. Are they saying something to me?

"Sagen sazoo wazen foo."

I think they're saying, "this song is for you!"

Without warning, they stopped. They didn't move. They didn't sing. They all looked up at the window, and stared at Ben.

In the quiet, he began to fidget and thought, why are they staring at me? Have I done something wrong? I didn't say a thing. I just stood here, crying and laughing. "Why are you looking at me. I'm just a little boy. I'm just Ben, you see," he pleaded.

Then, a creature with an oak tree planted high on his head, the largest of them all, took two long steps and stood facing Ben nose to nose through the window. Ben stepped back. It inched forward even closer. With the words crackling in his throat, Ben asked, "Who are you?"

The creature spoke softly, "Who are you?"

"Why, I'm Ben," he replied, his hands shaking.

"What are you?" the giant asked, furrowing his forehead and squinting as though he were trying to see Ben more clearly.

"I'm a little boy. A person," Ben said, matter of factly.

The huge chap laughed, then his face turned serious. "Ah, we know your type. You're the destroyers and the nurturers. The reapers and the wackers. The wrongdoers and the smackers. The list goes on, I'm sorry to say, but little do you know you're also a treemungerman, a flowerfang, a wiley wacky bushtock and a booly wooly snot tot." He laughed again, even louder.

Ben angrily stepped forward. "Don't you call me names. I'm none of those things!"

"Ahh," the creature said, "I don't call you names, I give you compliments just the same. Do you know who you are and where you come from? Little Ben, person and boy. It's grander than you can imagine. A story untold. We come to share it with you. You can save us, you know, but only if you're bold."

There was a gentleness about this huge fellow standing outside his window. Ben's fear began to melt, but he was still confused. Bewildered. Astonished. "What do you mean?" he said. "I'm just a little boy, you know. I couldn't save you. I wouldn't know what to do."

"Ah, I'm not so sure about that," said the huge oak, squinting again. "I see a giant in my eye, not a flea. But there is much to say and much to do. And the night is short. There's no time for stories about you. We need your ear for more important things, little Ben, treemungerman. Come down and stand with us for a while. Listen to our story. Listen to our plight. Listen to our song, then maybe you'll agree to set it right."

Ben was not sure. It was so late. What would his parents say? While he was debating back and forth, the giant with the oak on top of his head lifted the window with his big, rugged hand. He touched Ben on the cheek, not leaving a scratch. Ben's courage suddenly rose in his heart, and he said, "Yes! I'll come with you."

Without hesitating he climbed out the window onto the tree's limbs, and was whisked away as his shouts of glee rose to the heavens. High, high, higher he went. Towering over his house, he felt like a king looking down on the creatures from

5

Nowt. All the trees and bushes danced wildly, praising and singing his name, chanting, "Hah yah ho ya tane!"

The flowers waved in the breeze and chanted, "Ben, Ben, Ben be good. You are the one, the one who stood. For so long you protected us, and now you've returned. You've come home to carry this song, to see that the World of Nowt lives on."

Ben didn't understand a word of what they meant, but he didn't care. He was high in the trees, standing on a bent branch, looking out over the land. His eyes searched the forests, the pastures, and the hills as they stretched far away to the edge of night.

Then his knees began to shake. Never having been so high in the world, he suddenly felt scared. And, and he slipped. Ben reached out to grab a limb, but nothing was there, and he fell, and fell . . . but, before he hit the ground, an unusual sound whisked him back into the air. It was a whoosh. A wohl. A whirrh. It was wet but dry. It was the hand of the brook that ran beside the house! The hand of the brook that ran beside the house? Yes! The splash of a wave had saved his life.

He had never before seen the water dance, much less hold someone up in the air. Gently, it let him down. There he stood. A small thing. A speck. A mite. An ant among giants.

They gathered around him and sang. It was uproarious. Footsteps pounded. Huge boulders, named Sner-rocks, snored. The brook clapped its hands, mimicking the ringing crash of waves on the seashore. Marigolds crooned and buttercups swooned. Water lillies spun in the air, blowing bubbles as large as the trees. Ben began to sing and sway. He was bursting with excitement.

Without warning, like a thunderclap, the music died. The singing ceased. The dancing, clapping, and pounding stopped. It became so quiet he could hear his own breathing.

Ben whirled around. Paused. Then turned all the way around again, gaping at the smiling faces of the crowd gathered there. "Did I, I do something wrong?" he stammered.

"Hah, hah, hah!" They all laughed so hard that leaves shook from the tops of their heads and came raining down to the ground.

His friend with the oak on top stepped forward. "That depends upon your point of view, Ben," he said, as he stroked the tree roots that covered his chin like a beard. "Here in Nowt we see things different from you. Have you done something wrong? Maybe yes. Maybe no. It all depends on how you glow." Then he let out a mighty laugh, and the rest joined him, chuckling and holding their tummies.

"Good rhyme, old fella," said a willow creature as his branches whisked along the ground like a broom.

"I don't understand," said Ben. "It's you who invited me out to play, and I'm just a boy."

"Ah," said the giant to his companions, "he thinks he's just a boy, again!" Once more, they all burst out laughing.

Ben's eyes swelled with tears. He plopped down on the ground and began to sob, so strong that the trees and bushes started to fidget, and looked to each other with worried expressions on their faces. "Is he ill?" a poplar whispered to a pine.

The laughter faded. The oak giant reached down and touched Ben's cheek, caressing his head with the back of a leaf. Ben looked up, blinded by his tears. "Dear Ben, we mean you no harm or hurt. We forget how far away you've been from the dirt. Come, we must talk. We have much to teach you. To awaken memories of long ago, when you walked with us, forever bold. For you are chosen, chosen and few. We need you Ben to save this land. To reawaken the people of Luan. Time is short, and soon there may not be a day to precede the night. We'll be destroyed by those you call father and mother, sister and brother, neighbor and friend. They know not what they do. They are blind, and cannot see us, like you."

The great oak's words brought Ben's tears to a halt, and he felt light, as though the breeze were blowing right through him. In his heart, expectation welled up, but he didn't know why. "Am I dreaming?" he muttered.

"Dreaming? Oh no!" said the oak, as the brook splashed across Ben's face. "Have you ever felt or tasted water so real in a dream?"

Ben thought for a moment. "Well . . . no."

"Or," said a nearby pygmy creature with a rose bush climbing out of her ears, "have you ever smelled anything so delicious before this night? Have your eyes ever seen such a sweet sight?" She plucked a rose from her bushy head and waved it gently under Ben's nose.

"No," Ben replied.

"Well, then," said the giant oak, "don't let your fantasies and fears fool you, and don't let your heart harden to the wonders of this garden. All is true that you see and hear. All is more beautiful than anything you could fear. Now listen closely, for the night is almost over, and soon we must return to the earth's deep, dark cover. Another day is about to dawn. Our time is short and the words are many and long."

Ben listened without wavering an inch. He felt a kinship with these strange but lovable creatures, and yearned to hear every word they had to say.

The large oak sat down before Ben. "I am Scrawlyknot. We have waited long for you. Many a dew has come and gone. Many a spring has sprouted new growth, only to fall under winter's yoke. But now you sit before our Council of Nowt, and all that waiting has rewarded us with a new-found inspiration. It has brought you here before your friends, to hear our plight, and we hope, dear Ben, to make it right. But first I must ask you, are you ready to walk this road? Are you ready to carry the story of the world that is yet to be told? Dear Ben, to save the people of Nowt will require strength and courage, resolve to stand tall. It will be a lonely trek. But we will always be there for you. If you're willing to take this on, stand, follow us, and sing our song."

> Nowt, Nowt, our land of hope,
> I have come to save your fold.
> We stand together holding love,
> Forever bold.
>
> See coo wah hah nee
> Bu dov dee ree hee
> Ooh, ooh alahnee
> Fah, fah, hee, hee.
>
> See coo wah hah nee
> Bu dov dee ree hee
> Ooh, ooh alahnee
> Fah, fah, hee, hee.
>
> See coo wah hah nee
> Bu dov dee ree hee
> Ooh, ooh alahnee
> Fah, fah, hee, hee. . .

On and on the song went. Faster and faster the creatures danced. Up and down the flowers jumped, spinning like tops on a table. Ben's head began to weave and nod. Before long, he felt so tired, he couldn't even stand, and found himself lost in dreams that drifted by like clouds in the night.

Chapter 2

When sunshine broke through the clouds and splashed across his face, Ben opened his eyes and stared at the ceiling of his bedroom. He still wasn't quite awake, and his mind wandered as though he were dreaming. While yawning, he muttered under his breath, "See coo wah hah nee, bu dov dee ree hee. Ooh, ooh alahnee, fah, fah, hee, hee." Hmm, he thought, where did those words come from?

As quickly as the sun had shown its face, it disappeared. Rain began to fall. He jumped from the bed and ran to the window. It was a summer shower. Within moments the sun reappeared from behind a cloud, and every tree, bush, and blade of grass glistened.

Like that quick shower, memories of the previous night came rushing in. There was the giant oak, Scrawlyknot, who had lifted him from the room. The rose bushes that were growing from the ears of that wily fellow. The brook, who had saved him from crashing to the ground. He had never seen waters dance like that! And the wild beat of the creatures strumming their fingers against their tree trunks. Such sounds!

Yet, as he gazed out the window, the brook quietly flowed along the ground and into the woods. There was no song. No dance. No giants weaving tales. All that stood before him now were hills of grass and trees, the shed behind his house, the long drive leading to the road, and his old, rusty swing set.

Ben spoke through the window to no one in particular. "Was all that just a dream? Did it really happen? What about the rose I smelled and touched? Could that have been a dream, too?" Sad and dejected, he turned from the window. With his head downcast, he walked toward the door. On the floor were leaves still damp from the night's rain! On the bed, beside his pillow, was a rose freshly picked!

"It was real!" he yelled. The people of Nowt were not just a dream! What he had seen was true. He had to tell someone. "Wait till Mom and Dad hear about this!"

Clutching the rose in one hand and the leaves in the other, Ben ran down the stairs two at a time to the kitchen, and shouted at the top of his lungs, "Mom! Dad! Guess what happened last night! The trees came to life!" His parents looked up from the kitchen table, startled. Ben didn't even pause, but told them everything that happened. His mouth could hardly keep up with the words. "Scrawlyknot lifted me higher than the house, and the brook, it caught me when I fell, or I would have died. And this rose was on my bed this morning. The creature with bushes coming out of his head gave it to me. They called themselves treemungermen, and sang and danced. They even said I had been chosen to fight for them, to tell everyone about the destruction of Nowt."

Ben tried to catch his breath while his parents just stared at him. Finally his mother spoke. "Why honey, that's a lovely story. It's so imaginative."

"But Mom, it's not just a story, it really happened!" Ben stammered.

She paused for a moment and smiled, then reached over and pulled Ben into her arms. Hugging him tightly, she gave him a kiss on the ear. "I believe you, honey. Now, how about some breakfast?"

"Yeah, okay, Mom," Ben said, deflated.

She wore her favorite red-plaid apron, printed in white, "#1 Mom!" as she busied herself at the kitchen counter. Her brown, curly hair was pulled back in a pony-tail, and when she smiled her eyes crinkled up and looked like they were smiling too. While making Ben's breakfast, she hummed softly. Ben loved listening to her beautiful melodies.

All this time Ben's father sat silently with the newspaper folded in his lap. He was a slender man, and his hair was almost entirely grey even though he was not yet forty. Reading glasses were perched on the end of his nose, looking as though they might fall off at any moment. "Say, that was a great story, but I'd appreciate it if you'd tone it down a little the next time. You almost split my eardrums." He picked up the paper and began to read again. Ben collapsed into his chair, sulking, and picking at the rose and the leaves, wondering if the adventure with Scrawlyknot and the rosebush had been just a dream after all.

"Milk and honey on your oatmeal, dear?" his mother asked.

Ben stared ahead as though in a trance.

"Milk and honey on your oatmeal?"

"Oh, yeah," said Ben, all the while thinking of the events of the last evening. His mother placed the bowl of steaming cereal in front of him along with a plate of buttered cinnamon toast. Putting the rose and the leaves down on the table, he absentmindedly took the first bite of oatmeal, slurping the milk.

When he had almost finished, his mother yelled from the screen door in the back of the house. "Ben. Ben? Ben!"

"Yeah, Mom?"

"Zack's outside and wants to know if you want to play."

"Sure!" He got up from the table with a piece of toast still in his hand.

"First put some clothes and shoes on, and don't forget to brush your teeth!" she yelled after him as he ran up the stairs.

Nobody could put clothes on and brush teeth faster than Ben. Within two minutes he and Zack were running toward the woods behind the house, where the brook flowed.

His mother was busy cleaning up after breakfast. There on the table was Ben's rose. She put it in a thin vase filled with water and stuck it on the windowsill. "Honey, doesn't he have a wonderful imagination?" she said to her husband.

"Hmm, yeah." Ben's father continued to hide behind the newspaper.

"I don't know where he comes up with this stuff," she said almost to herself, heading for Ben's room to tidy up. She walked up the stairs slowly, lost in thought, talking out loud to herself. When she got to the door, she stopped. There on the carpet, leading from the open window to the bed, were muddy footprints. Walking over and sticking her head out, she looked down. "How on earth? It must be twenty feet to the ground." Then she remembered Ben's story over breakfast. Shaking her head, she thought, I'd like to hear what he has to say about this.

13

As she started to clean and straighten his room, her thoughts wandered off to all that needed to be done that day.

Meanwhile, Ben played outside with Zack who had moved into the farmhouse up the road just a few months earlier. He decided to keep the story of his friends from Nowt to himself for a while. If his parents didn't understand and believe him, maybe Zack wouldn't either. After all, he didn't want to be the butt of his friend's jokes.

Everything seemed so normal as they walked through the woods. Trees stood tall with roots firmly in the ground. There were no giants anywhere. Rose bushes just swayed in the breeze. The brook gurgled over rocks and moss. The forest had always been filled with mystery and adventure, but could there really be giants living in the ground under these trees? He wished they'd come out.

All morning he stared intently at everything, hoping to see a forehead, or maybe a paw. Nothing magic happened, though, and all he heard that day were the blackbirds singing.

That afternoon, Ben returned to the woods. All alone, he yelled, "Come out, come out, I'm Ben be good, I'm Ben who shook the tree and loudly stood!"

There was no answer. Only the wind whistled through the tree branches, crackling and rustling the leaves. The brook murmured softly.

He found a large boulder, a Sner-rock, which, the night before, had been alive. Now it just sat there, motionless. Ben squatted down on top of it, pulling his knees to his chest and holding his legs with his arms. At that moment, he felt as though he had lost something important, like a best friend.

Closing his eyes, he began to doze. During what seemed too real to be a dream, the Sner-rock Ben was sitting on rose out of the ground and cradled him in its arms. It sang him a lullaby, the same song that Ben learned the night before. "See coo wah hah nee, bu dov dee ree hee. Ooh, ooh, alahnee, fah, fah, hee, hee."

When Ben woke, not more than a minute or two later, he was muttering those verses under his breath. He reached down and awkwardly wrapped his arms around the boulder and kissed it. "I love you," he said.

At that moment a gust of wind blew through the trees and lifted Ben's gloom. He stood and yelled to the forest for all to hear, "I'm Ben, your friend! I'll protect you till the end." Then he jumped from the stone and danced and whirled like never before, chanting, "See coo wah hah nee, bu dov dee ree hee. Ooh, ooh, alahnee, fah, fah, hee, hee," as he spun from tree to tree. "Dos-e-doe and around we go . . . yeee heee!"

As though they were charmed, the trees swayed and rustled their leaves, singing, "Ben, Ben be good. You are he. You are here to set us free."

Ben screamed with delight, ran, and splashed in the stream. He lost track of time, caught, as it seemed, in a rhyme.

When the sun began to fall out of sight, his mother's call for dinner echoed through the woods. Ben stopped and fell to his knees, exhilarated! Taking a deep breath, he ran from the forest as fast as he could. Over the brook he leaped and across the field he sped until he stopped breathless at the back steps of his house.

Chapter 3

His mother was waiting for him. "My," she said. "You look happy. And are you dirty. Up to the bathroom right now and off with those clothes."

"Okay Mom." He leaped up the stairs, two and three at a time. Turning the knobs of the bath, he laughed to himself as the water came rushing out.

At the foot of the stairs his mother yelled, "Everything all right up there?"

"Uh, huh," he called down.

"Okay," she said doubtfully, returning to the kitchen.

When the tub was full he slipped in all the way up to his chin, closed his eyes, and thought about the day. Tonight, would it happen all over again?

His daydream was interrupted by his mother's knock on the door. She entered without waiting for an answer. "Here are some clothes. By the way, I noticed mud on your floor this morning. Did you go out before breakfast?"

He hesitated. "I told you, Mom, last night I was out with my friends from Nowt."

"Well, please wipe your feet next time before you track in dirt, okay? Now hurry and get dressed. Dinner's ready and your dad will be home any minute."

As she left, Ben pulled the plug in the tub and chuckled out loud as the water whirled down the drain.

At dinner, he was unusually quiet. His mother talked of her day, and his father spoke of the mall he was building, and how meddling officials were telling him which trees to cut, which to save, where to dig their ditches and dump their dirt.

Ben's heart ached as he listened to what his father was doing to the dirt. He had heard him speak before of his work, but now he listened with different ears. The sounds of trees falling and machines gouging the earth sent shivers crawling underneath his shirt.

"Daddy, why do you cut down the trees?"

"What do you mean, son?" His father arched his eyebrows.

"They're our friends you know. They can speak and feel just like you and me, and when you cut them they hurt, just as if you cut me."

His father silently pondered Ben's words. "Hmm," he said. "They speak, do they? Just what is it that they say?"

"Well, I'm not sure . . . just that they're dying and need our help."

"Maybe the trees do talk, but I can assure you they don't feel. And sometimes progress means cutting down a tree for something that's more important."

Ben listened quietly, but felt confused. After dinner he asked his mom if he could sit on the porch swing and watch the fireflies before going to bed.

"Alright. But just for a few minutes. You've had a long day."

He rocked back and forth watching the little bugs flashing in the night, chanting softly under his breath, "See coo wah hah nee, bu dov dee ree hee, ooh, ooh, alahnee, fah, fah, hee, hee."

Every time he sang, the fireflies lit up and danced about in circles. He couldn't help but giggle.

"Ben. Ben. Ben! his mother said louder until she got his attention.

"Oh. Yeah, Mom?"

"Time for bed."

"Okay," he said, reluctantly.

"What were you singing?"

"Oh, just something I made up."

"Hmm. Well, get ready for bed."

He whispered, "Good night, fireflies. I'll come and sing to you again, and you can dance for me. Remember, I'm your friend."

As Ben climbed the stairs he heard his mom say to his dad, "I don't know what's gotten into him today. From the first thing this morning he's been acting strangely. Did I tell you I found muddy footprints leading from his window to his bed? And the way he talked at breakfast and dinner!"

"There's nothing to worry about. He's as normal as they come," Ben's father said. "Now, do you want me to do the dishes or put Ben to bed?"

"I'll get the dishes. Besides, it would do you good to spend a little time with your son."

"You're right," he said, getting up to climb the stairs. As he sat down on the edge of the bed, he let out a deep sigh and ran his fingers through Ben's hair. "Do you want a story tonight?"

"Naw, that's okay, Daddy. I'm tired." With a yawn, Ben closed his eyes. Within a minute he slipped off to sleep. His father kissed him on the forehead and quietly left the room.

Ben slept in fits and starts, twitching and tumbling from one side of the bed to the other. In a dream, he was gathered with all his new found friends from Nowt. They sang and danced with abandon. Ben watched from the tallest limb atop Scrawlyknot's head. Without warning, Scrawlyknot shook, shuddered, and sneezed! The force sent Ben flying to the ground. As though he were a beach ball, he bounced back into the air and balanced on the tree's tiniest branch, which then tossed him to the tree-top. Back and forth they played with him as he giggled and spun through the air. Before he knew what had happened they had catapulted him to the tall grasses in the field below. Like a soft pillow, the long, green blades caught him so gently that he hardly felt the bump as he hit the ground. They rolled him up and down the hill beside his home, all the while tickling him under his chin.

He whirled and twirled like a top until he came to a stop at the edge of the brook. It rose up and floated in midair just as it had the night it saved his life. With the speed of lightning, it wrapped him like a mummy with sheets of water round and round and pulsed against his stomach.

As he laughed loudly, a gust of wind swooped down and lifted him into the sky beyond the earth, beyond his friends from Nowt, beyond the wet stroke of the stream. He could see the horizon, where the dawn of the day was just beginning. Golden rays of the sun peeked into the night.

Higher, higher still he went, riding a cloud into the dark reaches of space. He became lighter and lighter. When he looked down his body was still sitting beside the stream! Where he expected his body to be, he saw nothing more than a wisp of air in the shape of a little boy! There, whirling inside his chest, was the earth, right where his heart should have been. His eyes were like the stars in the heavens above. In his head wheeled the Milky Way.

In his belly, Ben felt new and odd sensations. Somehow, in his heart he knew everything that was happening in this world, from the swell of the ocean's tides crashing against a craggy shore, to people's laughter as they strolled down city streets. The sound of both rang in his ears.

But that was not all. When the earth's crust cracked from a quake deep in its core, he felt like his chest was rumbling. As mountains thrust higher into the sky, the thin air left him lightheaded and woozy.

Through his hands he could feel the scorching of man-made fires sweeping through ancient rain forests. His eyes burned with tears of sadness from the hot smoke.

Then a cloud's burst of rain cooled the fires, refreshing him. A single raindrop began to spread and stretch until it turned into the River Nile and overflowed its banks. Seeds that had been lying in the earth pulsed with new shoots of growth. Miraculously they became machines whirring in the night, changing into trains speeding like racing horses on rails, disappearing over the horizon.

With a sudden crash, an ax felling a tree sent a shiver up his spine. He wheezed and coughed from the choking air of cars' exhaust.

Ben screamed so loud he could be heard from one end of the universe to the end of his dream. Everything came to an abrupt standstill. A voice from deep in space pierced the silence.

"Ben, Ben, wake up."

He turned in its direction and yelled, "Help me! Help me!" But no sounds came from his mouth.

"Wake up. It's just a dream. I'm here." His mother cradled him, holding him close, sweetly kissing his forehead.

Through his tears Ben told her of the dream, of the worlds he'd seen. She listened quietly and intently.

"You mustn't worry. It's all been a bad dream, and in the morning you'll feel better. You'll see." She gently rocked him back and forth, back and forth. Slowly his eyes shut. When he was fast asleep and his breathing was heavy and regular, she pulled the covers up to his chin and sat watching him for the longest time.

Chapter 4

As Ben slipped off to sleep, he descended into a quiet, floating place. Once again, a sound called to him from far away. First he heard a clicking, then smooth familiar words. Softly at first, it drifted within ear shot, then grew louder.

"See coo wah hah nee, bu dov dee ree hee, ooh, ooh, alahnee, fah fah hee hee." Over and over he heard those familiar words beckoning from the darkness. With dream-eyes he saw the bright light of the moon silhouette a giant oak standing before his window. It was Scrawlyknot tapping the pane of glass with a branch, whispering that lovely chant. "Open your eyes," he said. "We have much to share, and the sun's about to rise. Open, open your eyes."

Ben woke and looked at the window. There stood the tree creature, just like in his dream! Scrawlyknot smiled and beckoned to him with his hand. "Hurry," he said. "There's much to do before the dread grows larger with the day's new dew."

Ben slipped from the bed, ran to the window, and opened it. Without saying a word, Scrawlyknot extended a branch. Ben climbed on and Scrawlyknot whisked him away.

Through the forest they dashed, then past the fields of farmer Collins' tall corn. On and on they strode until they reached the banks of the Cayhayu River. Into the rushing waters they waded with Scrawlyknot almost up to his chin. In a few moments, they climbed up the other bank.

Ben was standing so high in Scrawlyknot's branches he didn't even get wet. He screamed with excitement, "Ya hoo! Ya hoo!"

Faster and faster Scrawlyknot wended his way through the night air. Birds and animals called out from all sides. Scrawlyknot stopped, bellowing in a low, wispy voice. "See lah. See lah ho. Cooshe, megha, sandanchee so. Beera, coo shoo, coo shoo co."

Mice, foxes, does, and birds all spoke back with the most unusual words, "Hah shah, hah shah. Lee cantoo." It seemed as though the whole countryside was buzzing from the whispers of animals, large and small.

Onward Ben rode until he could see a soft glow of light through the canopy of trees. But this light was not from a fire or lamp. It seemed to float in the air, vibrant like the moon. Gathered all about it were beasts and birds, trees and rocks, and gurgling waters spouting like geysers into the sky. They all parted for Scrawlyknot and Ben, who stood in the fold of a branch.

As Ben and his great oak friend moved among them, everyone gathered there bowed down and chanted in a low rumbling sound, "Hah shah, hah shah, lee can too."

Scrawlyknot rumbled back, "Ben coo shoo, coo shoo, he can too." Then he lowered Ben to the ground.

Standing before that bright light, Ben felt as though it were blazing in his heart. With a sudden crack, like the sound of a tree falling in the forest, the light divided and half of it broke away and whirled around Ben's head. Faster and faster it spun, at a dizzying pace. Without warning, it stopped, right in front of his nose. Ben's head swooned and he felt faint, but Scrawlyknot reached down with his gentle hand to support him, holding him up with a loving touch.

The light began to buzz, crackle, sparkle, and fizz. Ben watched without blinking. But as quickly as the light had become almost electric, it got very quiet, and its glow started to die. Then, boom! It zoomed away into the night sky with a flash, until it could hardly be seen, and came rushing back faster than a rocket and splashed against his chest with an explosion! Some rays went right through his heart, but they didn't hurt. Some of them burst into a golden rainbow and wrapped around each animal, plant, and rock gathered there. It was as though the light streaming from Ben's heart was connected to each and every thing.

Ben stood as tall as any tree, smiling, his eyes gleaming brightly. He quieted the crowd with the authority of a grown man, not a boy. "I'm Ben, begotten, Ben be good. I'm the one who stood in the tree. I'll take a stand for all of you, for those who have passed and those to come, I'll protect you from all that's done. Thank you my friends of Nowt, from now on I will be your scout."

The treemungermen, the animals, the rocks, and the geysers shouted at the top of their lungs, "Ben begotten! Ben be good!" They raised their hands to the sky and danced with abandon.

After much merriment, Scrawlyknot held up his craggy hand to silence the throng. When the commotion subsided, he spoke, "Ben, you who stood among us for so long, we welcome your return. Your presence brings us great joy and raises our hopes. Walk in peace, uphold this land. Speak truth to the People of Luan. Teach them well. Lift the curtain from their eyes, that they may see unhindered by all those who lie. Remember, Ben, we are with you, always. In your sorrow, we are no farther away than tomorrow."

As he finished, the light hovering in the center of all those creatures of the earth slowly rose into the sky. In a way only spoken about in days of lore, it glimmered like a bright star in the night, seeming to rain down peace, joy, and comfort.

The whole Kingdom of Nowt sang, whistled, and romped to the beat of drums. Ben joined that dizzying throng. His head gyrated and his heart leaped. But soon everything blurred, and seemed to become foggy and faint.

He imagined that he was by the stream near his house, sleeping on a soft bed of moss with his hand stretched out over the water, which ran lightly over his fingertips. How strange it is to be dreaming this while I'm still dancing with my friends, he thought. Yet it seemed so real.

From the edge of the woods he heard a sound. Its vibrations rattled the ground and felt like the crashing footsteps of a giant. Closer and closer it came. With each thundering step it shouted Ben's name. In the dream he woke, and there was a huge treemungerman gently shaking him. It lifted him from the side of the stream where he slept.

"Ben, Ben. Wake up," it whispered into his ear.

Ben opened his real eyes wide and stared into the calm gaze of his father.

"You had your mom and me half worried to death, you know? Sleeping in the woods all night, with no blanket or anything, you could get pneumonia! What in the world were you doing out here?"

"Daddy, they came again for me last night, and we traveled to the Council of Beings. And light splashed right through my heart. We danced and sang, and I promised to keep them safe from the people of Luan, even people like mother and you."

His father looked at him with perplexity and worry in his eyes. He sighed. "Hmm. We better get you back inside and let your mom know you're safe. We can talk about your dream later, over breakfast."

As his dad clutched him in his arms and walked back through the woods, Ben said, "But Daddy, it wasn't a dream, it was real."

"I know," his dad said, patting him on the back as they walked into the yard. His mother was waiting at the kitchen door, and his father delivered Ben into her arms.

She knelt, holding him, crying. Ben cried too, but didn't know why. Lifting him she carried him up the stairs and plopped him on his bed.

Pulling his nightshirt over his head, she gasped. There on his chest, clearly etched, was an unusual mark. It looked like a star with hundreds of radiant arms. Faintly, on the skin surrounding the star, the colors of the rainbow softly glowed. She immediately put her hand to his forehead to feel for a fever, touched his chest, then rubbed at the star. It wouldn't come off. With each touch it glowed more brightly.

Irritated, she said, "What have you been doing? How did you paint this on your chest? Don't you know putting things like this on you could poison you?" With every word she got more upset.

"I didn't paint it, Mom. It's like I told Dad, at the Council of Beings the light splashed through me and must have left this mark." Then Ben touched his chest. "Wow!"

Ben's mom grabbed him by the shoulders and shook him. "This is no joke. You can't go sleeping in the woods and painting stars on your chest. These stories, they're just dreams! Now stop all this nonsense!"

Amid tears and sobbing, all he could say was, "The tree, it must've left me in the woods. They're not lies and dreams, they're real. They're real, I swear it!"

She breathed deeply, composing herself. "Get dressed and come down for breakfast. We'll talk this over with your father." She turned and left the room, leaving Ben crying. He had never felt so lost and alone in all his life.

Who would believe him? How could he make people see that the trees were alive, that they speak and feel just like humans? If his parents wouldn't listen to him, how could he defend his friends from Nowt? He was just a little boy. Who would care? He stared through the window with tearful eyes at the great oak standing tall.

Chapter 5

O ver breakfast everyone sat in silence for a long time. Then Ben's father cleared his throat while folding his hands on the table. "You know, when I was younger than you, I, too, used to play in the woods behind our house. I have such happy memories of that time. I even had friends that no one else could see." Ben's face lit up. "That's right. We would sing and dance and play all day. So, you see, I understand how you've been feeling. But when you get to be nearly eight years old, it's time to say goodbye to all your fantasy friends. It's time to stop all the imagining and begin dealing with the world as it is. Do you understand, son?"

"But Daddy, I'm not a liar. These things really happened to me!"

"I know it seems that way. It's okay, but these are just make-believe friends. And another thing, I don't want you sleeping in the woods again. Do you understand?"

"Yes, Daddy." Ben looked down at the table top, his chest sunken like a heavy weight was resting on it.

"Good. Now I'm late for work and have got to be running." He kissed Ben's mom on the forehead, patted Ben on the head, grabbed his briefcase, and went out the door.

Ben's mother went into the den to finish reading the paper, leaving Ben alone with his thoughts. He was confused and didn't know what to do. Looking blankly at the cereal bowl, he nibbled on his dry toast.

From the other room his mother called, "Why don't you go see if Zack can play? It's beautiful out."

"Okay, Mom." Ben cleared his dishes to the sink. Sitting on the sill in full bloom was the rose from yesterday's adventures with his friends from the Kingdom. As he turned to leave the kitchen a glow of light streamed from the petals and splashed against his back. If he had seen it he would have known why his dark mood mysteriously lifted at that very moment. Running from the kitchen and through the back door, he sang at the top of his lungs. "See coo wah hah nee bu dov dee ree hee. Ooh, ooh, alahnee, fah, fah, hee, hee!"

Hearing him, his mother stopped her work. Those strange words again, she thought. I hope nothing's wrong with my little boy. Picking up where she left off, she began absentmindedly whispering, "See coo wah hah nee bu dov dee ree hee. . . ."

As Ben ran through the backyard, he stopped. Standing in front of him was the big oak, his friend, his ally, the one who carried him so tall across the river and beyond to the gathering around that mysterious light.

Ben reached out his hand and ran it down the tree's trunk, then hugged Scrawlyknot as best he could. "I hope you come visit me tonight. I have so many questions I want to ask you."

Kissing the tree with a big smack of the lips, he let out a loud "Whoopie!," then ran off to Zack's house across the field.

Without him knowing it, his mother stood at the window, watching and worrying about her little boy. She thought, is it normal for little boys his age to hug, talk to, and kiss a tree goodbye? Perhaps I should speak to Dr. Sanders about all this.

That day Ben and Zack played by the brook. They ran through the forest in search of pirates and hidden gold, and ate peanut butter sandwiches that Zack's mom had neatly packed into brown paper bags. In the late afternoon when the sun turned red, floating just above the top of the trees, Ben said goodbye to his friend and headed home.

At dinner, his dad spoke of how they had cleared the land for more buildings and parking lots.

Ben innocently asked, "Who said you could do that?"

"We get permits from the county. Why?"

Ben scowled.

"You're worried about the trees, aren't you? There are still plenty of trees around."

"No there aren't!" Ben said defiantly. "They're dying. When the treemungermen hear about this they're going to be so sad."

"Treemungermen?"

Ben nodded matter-of-factly.

"Hmm," his father grunted. "Well your treemungermen don't have to earn a living. Now finish your dinner so you can get ready for bed."

Ben wanted to say or do something, but didn't know what. After picking at his food until it was cold, he told his mother that he was full. She suggested that he play in his room before going to bed.

At the top of the stairs, Ben turned and sat down. Below, his parents were whispering. "You didn't have to be so hard on him," bristled his mother.

"Who's being hard? He has to learn to get these strange ideas out of his head," his father shot back.

"It's just that he seems to be so sensitive right now. He treats the trees like they're his best friends. I think it hurts his feelings when he hears what you do."

All Ben heard was silence for a few moments. Finally, his father spoke up. "It gets under my skin when I work my brains out all day and come home and have my son look at me as though I'm practically a murderer for cutting down a few trees." He sighed. "I'll say something to him before he goes to sleep."

His mother yelled up the stairs from the kitchen. "Ben, it's getting late. Time to get ready for bed."

When his father poked his head in the bedroom door, Ben was already under the covers with a dinosaur book resting on his chest. He had been scouring the pages for a picture of a treemungerman. There weren't any.

"May I come in?" Ben nodded. Sitting down, he placed his big hand on Ben's chest. "It's hard being a little boy, isn't it? I'm sorry I was so tough on you at dinner. It's just . . . that, I want you to know that people who cut down trees are not bad. Me included. I care about trees too, but you see there's this thing we call progress, and sometimes trees get in the way. We try to save them and plan around them. But often we can't avoid it."

"But Dad, they're dying. The world, it's dying, and if we don't save it, it's not going to make it. Don't you see?" Tears welled up in his eyes and he began to sob. His dad pulled him close and held him silently. His eyes grew moist, too.

They held each other for the longest time, until Ben's sobs and tears were replaced with the deep breath of sleep. His dad lowered him back to the pillow and sat there for a few minutes, watching his face.

Hearing a strange noise from outside, he turned and looked through the window. He thought he saw something out of the corner of his eye, but it was only the great oak, quietly blowing in the breeze. It was the beauty of that tree that made him want to build a house here. With a heavy sigh, he lifted himself from the bed and tiptoed out of the room, pulling the door nearly closed behind him.

In the den below, Ben's mom was curled up on the couch, reading a magazine. She looked up. "Everything all right?"

"Sure, he's going to be fine."

"Are you okay? You look like you've been crying."

"Yeah, yeah, I'm fine. Something your son said really moved me. He's a very sensitive kid. Want some tea?"

She nodded, and her eyes followed him as he continued to the kitchen. He had never felt the way he felt at that moment. The things Ben said made him uncomfortable. Busily pouring the boiling water, dipping tea bags in cups, and squeezing the honey bear, he left behind thoughts of his son and trees, and his mind wandered off to all he had to do the next day.

Chapter 6

In the middle of the night, almost like clockwork, came a tap, tap, tapping at Ben's window. He was lost deep in sleep. Groggy, and not sure where he was, he opened his eyes, took a deep breath, let it out, then slipped from the covers. As he walked to the window he could see Scrawlyknot standing there, tall and stout, with shiny, white teeth showing through his big smile. Ben pulled the window up, still dreamy.

"My," the great oak said, "you must have been traveling far away in Nanterland. I didn't think you were ever going to wake up."

"Nanterland?" Ben asked.

"The land you people call dreams. Actually, it's just the hinterlands of the Kingdom of Nowt."

"What's a hinterland?"

"You know, the outskirts. Someday we can go there together. But tonight, my friend, you and I must travel a different road. I've come to speak of the time when the people of Luan sank their roots way down below the dew. Here, stand on my branch, and we'll find a clearing in the field of corn where we can sit quietly, and adorn your history with words of love and loss, when you were tossed from your home in the sun's bright light, scorned and torn. Hurry, there's much to say, and the sun's glory is not far away."

Ben climbed aboard and held tight to Scrawlyknot's trunk. Off they marched into the crisp night air.

When they entered the corn field, Scrawlyknot brushed back the tall husks and gently placed Ben on the ground. He whistled, and a large Sner-rock scampered to his side and spoke in a strange tongue. "Yee koo ooo, yee koo ooo."

Scrawlyknot replied, "Yak a aha, yak a aha," and the large boulder sat down squarely behind Ben, giving him a place to rest his back. Ben nestled into a crease in the rock. It fit him perfectly. Then, Scrawlyknot squatted down in front of him and crossed his legs, creaking with every bend.

"Oh, I'm getting too old to sit on the ground. You know, standing is much easier for me. But I want to get close. I want you to hear every sound." Leaning forward, he touched his nose to Ben's nose.

Ben flinched back, surprised.

"Don't be frightened."

"Oh, I'm sorry. It's just . . . your nose is so big!"

"And yours is so small, but it suits you well."

Ben reached up self-consciously to feel his nose.

"Noses are such wonderful things, you know. In fact, touching noses is an old custom we treemungermen use to start conversation of a lofty kind." He patted his chest. "It reminds us of our deep ties, and that truth must always be spoken from the heart." Scrawlyknot patted his chest. Your Eskimos still use this ancient custom. They learned it from us ages ago when people and trees conversed and shared knowledge of the universe."

"The Eskimos knew the treemungermen?"

"Yes, my dear Ben, there was a time when trees and the people of Luan were friends, not enemies."

Scrawlyknot's eyes filled with tears. A large one rolled down his face, falling with a big splash on Ben. To Ben, it tasted salty like the ocean. The great oak sobbed. "My friends, my brothers, my sisters, you must do what you can." He lifted his gaze to the stars. His sad lament filled Ben with sorrow. He, too, cried. Holding each other's hand, they sat for what seemed to be an endless time. When the tears slowed to a trickle, Scrawlyknot spoke again.

"Our time is short, and I have many things to say. I'm not sure where to start. You see, much has happened since the Great One pulled back the veil on this world, breathed life into you and me, and separated the light from the dark. Did you know there was a time when you and I were like cousins?" Scrawlyknot didn't wait for Ben's reply. "We rose in the darkness from the same spark, and stood in the ground, tall and true, blowing in the gentle winds of the land we once called Ranu. Oh, we were different, but so much the same. Together we conversed with one eye on the Holy One above, and one on the ground below. There was no fear then, only love. No hate of race, no call to destroy or deface. There was plenty for all, and more, for all those who follow His law." Scrawlyknot paused, looking off into the distance, as though he saw all that he described unfolding before his eyes.

"For reasons I cannot explain, things changed. No one knew why. There was no sign from even the sky. In the early hours one day, the men and women of Luan decided not to stay. They learned they could walk in the sun, whereas we could only walk in the night. At first, they always returned to us, the treemungermen, when the dark veil fell over the land. But soon their wandering carried them farther and farther from our forest home. They journeyed across the sands and dunes beyond the reaches of our time and our love."

"What did they look like?"

"Oh, much like you, except their skin was coarser, more weathered. And their arms looked like branches. Some even had leaves."

"What happened to them when they left?"

"They were gone for many generations. Each of us had children, and our children had children by the score. Unfortunately, the day came that we knew each other no more. When the people of Luan returned to the land of the treemungermen, we stood silent out of fear. They had become so strange! No longer did they look like us. And their customs were foreign. Their words were strident and full of hate. And they brought with them new companions—fire and ax! They attacked us for our wood with a vengeance, and didn't even ask. Pain rang out through the earth and hardened the hearts of the treemungermen."

"So, my dear Ben, for the longest time we have not been friends. Of course, there have been a few among you with redeeming hearts, who have been kind to us, and prevented people from lopping off our tops. Just the same, we have not felt safe to play and dance in the open air until you came to us as told in the prophecy of long ago—a child of Luan will bring back life to every treemungerman. He will plant himself beside us, and grow tall, his spirit rising and changing the air for all. His words will shake forests, stopping monsters in their tracks. The lakes will again sparkle, and all who stand beneath his limbs will marvel."

"How do you expect me to do all that? I wouldn't know where to start."

Scrawlyknot looked deeply into Ben's eyes. "Even though you are young, your spirit is very, very old. You were here in the beginning, as it is told."

"But I'm only seven!"

"Yes, that is true. But every treemungerman knows that souls can be much older than their bodies."

Ben silently tried to comprehend what this meant.

"When we heard of your return, the skies cleared. We have been waiting patiently for you to grow and learn. You are no ordinary child. You're a relative of the treemungermen, remembered for your kindness of heart, and wisdom to know when to stop, and when to start. You have been sent to us to fill the Luanian chests with hearts that beat and feel; that know how to touch and be touched; that recognize truth and beauty, and what is just. This is no easy task, and it's much to ask of a child. But I promise you'll find a strength that will well up from the soles of your feet and surge through every vein."

"I've never felt anything like that in the soles of my feet!"

"Ah, you will. But that's all I can say this night. Now you must return and into your dreams will seep all I have uttered. My words will set your heart ablaze with a compassion that will change this world for all days."

With dreary eyes, Ben tried to protest, but he was too tired. Scrawlyknot lifted and carried him into the woods by his house. Softly, he set him down by the gurgling stream. The lovely music of the water quietly wove its way into his sleep.

In the morning, as the sun rose, Ben woke, cold, yawning, reaching for covers that weren't there. "Oh no, I've slept in the woods again!" Running with bare feet, he jumped across the stream, scurried through the backyard and up the stairs without a sound, and slipped into bed.

Chapter 7

It had only been a few minutes when his dad gave him a light shake. "Get up Ben. Are you awake?"

"Yeah Dad, I'm up," he said, as he faked a big yawn.

At breakfast, Ben slouched over the table with droopy eyelids. Wearily, he ate his cereal.

"Anything wrong?" his father asked.

"I didn't sleep well last night."

"Well, even though it's Saturday I was going to go in to work for a few minutes and check on the site. The men are working 'round the clock. But if you're too tired to go in with me this morning . . ."

Ben perked up. "Oh, no. Can I go please, pretty please? Can I get up on one of the tractors, too?"

"I think we can arrange that. But you'd better finish your cereal and get dressed. I've got to be there by nine."

Ben gobbled down the remainder of his breakfast and leaped up the stairs. In a flash he was back waiting by the door.

"Aren't you going to tie your laces?" His father surveyed him from head to foot.

"I'll do it in the car."

After a quick goodbye to his mom, Ben and his dad were riding down the county road. As they drove, more and more houses appeared. More buildings. More cars. More noise. The air began to smell from the smog.

"Does it always smell so bad here, Daddy?"

"Oh, I don't know. I guess I really never noticed it. But yes, it does."

After a while they turned down a dirt road. On each side were cranes, big tractors, and gigantic machines pushing the earth back and forth.

"Why are they smoothing out that dirt over there?"

"That's where the parking lots go," he said, matter of factly.

"But how will the earth breathe?"

"Breathe?" His father furrowed his forehead.

"Yeah, and it won't be able to feel the sun either."

"Well . . . I don't think you need to worry about these things. They'll be all right."

They rode the rest of the way in silence. When they reached the trailer where his father worked, Ben asked if he could play outside. His father said okay, but that he would need to stay in the fenced area. Ben agreed.

Running to the fence, he clutched it with his fingers, watching intently. Machines with wheels that seemed to be bigger than his house roared by. Just beyond the dirt road stood a man wearing a helmet. He was shouting orders above all the noise to other men with helmets, and to a man driving a huge tractor. The workmen were dragging heavy chains over their shoulders. They hooked them to trees one by one and the tractor roared and puffed black smoke like a dragon, prying them from the ground. Their cracking and severed roots gave off ear-splitting screams. Ben felt horrified.

"No! No! No!" he shouted.

His tiny voice couldn't be heard above the din of the machinery. No one was paying enough attention to see the tears streaming from his eyes. He looked around for someone to help, but there wasn't anyone, and no one seemed to care. Without thinking, he darted across the dirt road, dodging large equipment. Down the dirt embankment he ran right into the middle of the workers.

"Stop it! Stop it! You're killing them! Don't you know there are treemungermen under there and they can't breathe and live without the trees?"

As though he were a mighty general, he brought them to a standstill. They stood motionless and stared at this little boy. The tractor belching black smoke came to a halt, too. Its engine slowly wound down until it was silent. The men looked at one another, unsure of what to do.

The man who had been shouting orders walked over to Ben. "Who are you, son?"

"Why, I'm Ben begotten, Ben be good, I'm the protector of these trees."

The foreman looked up at his fellow workers and shrugged his shoulders. Ben continued to stand defiantly in his way.

"Young fellow, I don't know who you belong to, but we got work to do here. You best be getting back across the road and find your dad."

Ben stood his ground. "You're not cutting down any more trees. The people of Nowt have asked me to save them. So I'm telling you, stop it!"

"Or what?" the foreman laughed. The rest of the men smiled and laughed, too.

"Or . . . or . . . Scrawlyknot will come here and kill all of you."

"Whoa now son," said the foreman, grabbing Ben by the arm. But Ben broke free from his grip and ran into the middle of the stand of trees. Taking hold of a low limb, he began to climb until he was soon out of reach, and almost out of sight. The foreman cursed Ben, then looked around at the blank and waiting faces of the rest of the workmen. "Bob," he said, "run to the office and tell Jim Krantz we got a problem out here. And see if you can find out who this boy belongs to!"

Ben sat there, nearly forty feet up, staring down at the men. He felt so scared that he shook and his heart quaked in his chest. Holding onto the tree trunk for dear life, he thought, what will I say to dad? He'll be mad.

Down below, more men were gathering as word spread about the defiant young boy up in a tree. They all wanted to see who had stood up to Joe Killingham, the toughest foreman on the site, and given him a tongue-lashing!

When Ben's father arrived he broke through the crowd, looked up, and shouted. "Is that you, Ben?"

A faint whisper of a voice came calling down. "Yes, Daddy."

"I want you out of that tree right now!"

For the longest time there was silence. Ben was thinking about what to do. "Only if they promise not to cut down any more trees!"

His father turned red in the face. "If you don't come down right now young man I'll be cutting down more than trees!"

"Then I'm not coming down!"

The men laughed. His father turned and faced them. Many of them sheepishly looked to the ground. "It's time the rest of you men got back to work." Turning to the foreman, he said, "Why don't you find something else for your men to do, but be prepared to continue clearing this afternoon."

"What about your son?" the foreman asked as he looked up.

"Don't worry, you just get your men out of here and I'll get him down."

The men walked off in different directions, many of them heading for the planning trailer for a cup of coffee and a donut. By chance, one called his wife, and in passing, mentioned what had just happened.

Ben's dad stood there, thinking, breathing deeply. He was angry and confused, and didn't know what to do.

"Ben, why are you doing this?" he shouted, barely able to see his son as he hid among the branches.

Ben didn't answer.

"Ben!"

"Because of the trees, Daddy. If you cut the trees down all the creatures under the earth will die."

Ben's dad ran his hand through his hair and looked at the ground. "What creatures?"

"The ones that come to visit me every night. I promised them I'd do everything I could to protect them. They chose me, Daddy, and no one else."

His father sighed and shook his head. The anger drained from his voice. "Ben, you have to come down. You can't stay up there. Come on, son, and we'll talk about it," he coaxed.

"Not until you promise that you won't cut any more trees."

"I can't promise that. It's not mine to say. But I will talk to them and see if we can save some trees, all right?"

"No, then I'm not coming down."

"Ben, I've never seriously lost my temper with you, but if you don't come down this instant I'm going to give you a spanking like you can't imagine."

Ben was silent.

After waiting for another minute, Ben's dad, fuming, spun around, kicked up the dust, and marched off in the direction of the construction office. When he got to the gate, he yelled to the foreman who had been watching from a distance. He spoke a few words, then kept walking.

All the while Ben surveyed the countryside from his high perch as he held the tree closely with his arms. His little body was still shaking. He had never made his dad so mad. How could he make him understand his promise to protect his friends from Nowt?

Without him knowing it, a large bird circled above him, in and out of the clouds. Turning his eyes to the sky, he saw it and wished he were flying, too. Why had they chosen him to protect the trees? Why did he have to get into so much trouble with his dad?

A sudden gust of wind made the tree sway. As if by magic, all of his doubts, questions, and worries faded. Ben decided that if he must, he'd stay.

The day wore on. Occasionally he'd see his father step outside and look his way, then return to the trailer shaking his head. The men went about their work, ignoring him and the stand of trees.

Ben wondered how long he could stay up there. He was hungry, and his bottom and legs were sore from sitting on the hard limb for so long. Would he spend the night? How would he sleep? Maybe he should believe what his father said, that if he came down, everything would be all right.

As his doubts grew, the bird that had been circling above whooshed by his nose and settled on a branch just below. Ben sat quietly, watching, afraid to move. He had never been so close to such a large bird. It was a beautiful peregrine falcon. Out of its head grew a white plume, and its feathers glistened in the light.

With a sudden flurry, the bird spread its wings and with one flap, came to rest on the branch next to Ben. Staring straight ahead, it closed its eyes and settled down for what seemed to be a nap. Ben held his breath, but wasn't scared. He had danced and sung with birds at the Circle of Beings. Still, to be so close to such a magnificent creature in the light of day! He could hear the bird's wheezing lungs. When the wind blew, its feathers ruffled. Yet he just sat, and sat, and sat with his eyes closed.

Ben became drowsy. His eyelids grew heavy. He was drifting off to sleep when a tug on his shirt and a high-pitched voice woke him. "Watch out now, or you'll fall." Ben jerked awake, shocked. He looked below, but there was no one there who could have spoken to him. He was sure he'd heard someone say something. Could it be the bird?

"Did you say something?" he asked.

"Who else?" said the bird. "The wind blowing through your clothes, I suppose?"

Ben was wide-eyed. "It's just, I just never spoke, I . . . ."

"I know, I know," squawked the bird. "But times are different now. I've decided I'd like to be heard."

"Are you friends with the great oak tree?"

"Of course I'm friends with Scrawlyknot. Who else would send me to waste my time speaking to a featherless creature like you, if it wasn't for the fact you're the one who's been chosen?"

"Well, you don't have to be so nasty," Ben shot back.

"Nasty? My little friend, be careful how you speak, or I'll peck you with my beak." Then he made a motion with his snout in jest, and Ben nearly jumped out of the tree. The bird laughed and chattered so loud he could be heard for miles away. "Cha, cha, cha, cha . . . ."

Ben snapped back, "Are you making fun of me?"

"No, no, I was just having my daily laugh you see. Because when I laugh, my troubles seem to fade. I can see by looking at your face, my friend, you could use a laugh, too. In your eyes I see worry to no end."

"Well, yes, I am. You'd be worried too if you didn't do what your father said, and stayed up in a tree."

"Hmm, fathers can be a problem, especially if they don't understand the woods, and the troubles they sow. Still, we have a job to do, and I've come to keep you company, to be certain your spirit does not bend."

"But, what's going to happen to me? I can't stay here forever."

Taking the tip of his wing and stroking his chin, his feathered friend said, "Some great things do take forever. For example, our Creator, he's still trying to make our world, always

48

looking for something better. But people, they get in the way, and don't know how to play. They'd rather search for glory and fame, move the earth, and make the wilderness tame. They're much too busy with their ideas to ever notice a bird or a twig, much less a boy resting on a limb in a tree. You've done the right thing, following your heart even when the voices within you fought. We may be here a while, and I've come to comfort you, even make you smile."

Ben grinned and reached out to stroke the feathers of his new friend. Then he withdrew his hand, twisting his face with worry again. "But what about food and water. I'm already thirsty."

"Ah, don't you be troubling yourself with such insignificant matters. We'll take care of you and see that you drink from the morning dew, from the arms of friends who will give their life to you."

Without saying another word, the great falcon sprang into flight and disappeared, leaving Ben wondering. Then the bird reappeared, landing softly next to him. In her beak was the arm of a cactus, dripping and wet.

"Stick this in your mouth and suck it dry. It'll quench your thirst."

Reluctantly, and carefully, Ben took it and began to suck, and sweet water dripped down his lips. He had never tasted anything so good. He sucked, and sucked, and sucked the cactus dry.

The falcon said, "Say 'thank you'."

"Thank you." Ben nodded to the falcon.

"Not to me, silly, the cactus!"

"The cactus?"

"Of course, the cactus. Did it not give you all its water, and its limb to boot. Have you not learned anything yet?"

49

Ben turned to the cactus, and said haltingly at first, "Thank you cactus for quenching my thirst. I don't know what I would have done without you."

"That's better! You see, everything in mother earth should be thanked, because without the earth we could not fly, and it's through the earth that we are born and die. It's in the thanking, you see, that we find ourselves again, indeed."

Ben quizzically asked, "What do you mean?"

"Well, um." The falcon paused for a moment, deep in thought. "Everything has a spirit. You, me, even the cactus and the tree. When the Great One breathed that spirit into the tree, he thanked it, just for being. And He treasured it, just because it gave him so much pleasure. So it is with all the world. By thanking each thing, we raise it high and make it a treasure in our eye. A world that's treasured can never truly be measured for cutting and digging. In the Kingdom, we call that sinning."

". . . uh, I don't even know your name."

"You may call me Pere."

"I see. Well, thank you, Pere, and air and tree for supporting me, and giving me breath. Thank you for being my friends. I'll try to always protect you."

The falcon nodded in approval, then stretched its wings. "I'll be back, hold this tree to your heart." He lifted up with one flap of the wings, hovered in midair, then said, "See coo wah hah nee!" Soaring into the sky, he was gone from sight within less than a minute.

It was now afternoon. Ben's father sat in his office wondering what to do about his stubborn son. Should he call his wife? Perhaps his son was right? But what could he do? Whether those trees stood or were to be cleared was not his department. It's what the plans called for anyway. They had to be pulled out to make room for parking. The whole area was meant to be open and bright. No, he thought. There was nothing to be done.

Without him knowing it, the wife whose husband mentioned the stand-off between boy and man called another friend, and mentioned it in passing. Sure enough, that friend called another friend, and so it went that word of this strange little boy's act of disobedience spread throughout the town as though carried by the wind. Finally, every reporter within fifty miles descended upon that building site with lights, cameras, helicopters, and all sorts of contraptions imaginable to determine why a little boy was up a tree, and a construction site had come to a standstill.

When Ben's dad saw them coming, he buried his head in his hands and moaned. How could this day get any worse? How was he going to face his wife?

They broke through the door of his dad's office with cameras rolling, flashes flashing, and together they roared, "What's this about a boy in a tree? Are you his father? What does he want? Is he stuck? Can we get our truck down there? Where's his mother? Does she know? Why are you tearing down the trees anyhow? Why don't you just leave them in a row?"

Ben's dad raised his hands to calm the crowd. His lips were pursed and his fists were clenched. He tried tranquilly to explain that this was a family matter, and none of their concern. It was not so absurd, just a young boy disobeying his father. He would come down soon, so why all the bother?

Being good reporters, they were not deterred. One piped up and said, "Let's have a look at the boy, talk with him, and see what he has to say." Out they rushed with Ben's father running behind, toward where Ben sat resting in the breeze.

"Heh, young man, are you stuck?" shouted an older fellow with a bushy moustache.

"Why did you climb the tree?" yelled a young woman with a long ponytail. Fast and furious they all started asking questions without even pausing for answers.

"What can you see?"

"Why did you disobey your father?"

"Are you still hot under the collar?"

"Is it true you won't move until your father agrees to stop cutting trees?"

"Are you hungry?"

"Are you thirsty?"

"Are you lonely?"

"How long do you plan on staying up there?"

"Will you come down if your father gives in?"

Ben tried his best to answer each of their questions, but the more he said, the more they asked.

"You said trees speak to you, and told you to stay?"

"The earth will die if we don't take a stand?"

On and on they went. On and on Ben answered. Each time he received a compliment.

"Such a bright boy."

"He does make some sense you know."

"To do what he suggests is going to cost these people a lot of money."

As the questions flew by, Ben's dad sat on a fallen tree, with his head in his hands.

To make matters worse, people started calling into the office, as far away as River Falls.

"The boy is right, you know!"

"We won't shop in your mall if you cut down those trees!"

Throughout the day the callers kept the phones busy letting Ben's dad know what they had on their minds. Finally, he got a call from a woman frantic and screaming.

"What are you going to do?"

"Well I . . ."

"If you leave my son up in that tree I'm not sure I want to be married to you!" She said "good-bye" after she had already slammed the phone down. Ben's mother collapsed on the overstuffed couch in the living room and cried. She had just heard the news on the radio moments before.

Ben's dad had tears in his eyes, too. With a heavy heart and a sigh, he walked down to the trees, through the throng of reporters, and looked up at Ben. "All right. You win. I won't cut down any more trees. You can come down now."

Ben smiled. Turning to the tree, he thanked it for its support, its branches, its limbs, its leaves, its swaying in the breeze. He kissed it and took one last look out over the valley before he placed his foot on the branch below. As he stepped down, the tree shook violently. Scared, he withdrew his foot, and the tree stopped shaking. At first, almost beyond the reach of his hearing, he heard a whisper.

"Do not go yet. Yana foo rehooray net. We need you here for one night more."

Ben stuttered, "But . . ."

"Ah, I know what you think. If you feel you must go, then do so now. But if you stay, you can help the world in ways you cannot imagine." The tree fell silent.

"Dad!"

"Yes, son."

Hesitantly, Ben called down. "I've decided to stay the night."

"You can't sleep up there!"

"Oh yes I can, it'll take care of me."

"But Ben . . ."

"No Daddy, I'll be all right. I promise you I'll come down first thing in the morning."

Ben's dad looked at the ground and kicked a small stone, and bit his upper lip.

"What am I going to tell your mother? She's worried sick."

Ben paused and thought. With pride, he said, "Tell her . . . tell her I'm Ben begotten, Ben be good, Ben who stands for trees and shores long forgotten. I'm her son, but much more."

His father was overwhelmed. More and more he was filled with a deepening doubt. Yesterday, Ben was just a little boy playing. Now he's acting like a prophet, persuading the crowd, commanding their attention. This wasn't the voice of a child. He marveled at his son, yet feared for something he could not even describe.

Lovingly, he said, "Ben, I want you to know how dear you are to me. I'm really concerned for your safety. It's a long way up and I don't want you falling in the night. Please Ben, I ask you, come down. Let's end this silly fight."

Ben pleaded. "Dad, can't you see. I have to stay. You've gotta understand."

The reporters began buzzing. It was a good story for the six o'clock news. With cameras rolling they said they would continue their vigil into the night to see if anything would happen before the next day. His father turned and walked back to the office to call Ben's mother. He was mulling over how he could explain why their son would not come down. As he talked, she listened silently. He finished by saying, "Please bring me my sleeping bag, thermos, and flashlight." He too would camp out and watch over his son that night.

As dusk rolled in, the sky greeted the crowd of reporters and onlookers with a crimson and golden show of splendor. For a few moments, all eyes turned to the West, captured as in a dream, transfixed by a beauty beyond anything they had ever seen. Then those bright hues turned softly to grey. The darkness of the night descended and all was quiet.

Chapter 8

As Ben peered into the thick darkness, he could hardly see the outline of people moving about. Occasionally the flicker of a flashlight lit up the face of a man or a woman and then it was gone. As the night progressed, fireflies flashed here and there, and the whole world below seemed like the sky, filled with stars, aglow.

Ben nestled further into the crook of his branch, feeling quite hungry. He wished that his friend, the peregrine falcon, would return with food. If he could just have an apple or a pear, something to tide him over.

In his mind he began calling the falcon. His eyes searched the night intently for something in flight. After a few moments he could hear the flapping of wings. His spirits rose. He called, "Pere, is that you?" The tree rustled and shook, and the great wind of wings blew Ben's hair back as a large bird descended on the branch next to him.

Standing before him, though, was not the falcon! It was an eagle bigger than Ben. Its eyes gleamed in the night and its head was white as snow.

As it folded its wings it chanted. "Sah yah harh woo hooo, Ben lah ho lah doo. Ahziz ruhr, caliz duhr. Antai yo, antai yo. Yee cohr rie, lisso mee. Yom!" Then in a deep throaty voice, it said, "See now if you can sing it."

Ben was so disarmed by this unexpected visitor and his beautiful song, he just went along. He tried singing it with the great eagle's help. "Sah yah harh woo hooo, Ben lah ho lah doo. Ahziz ruhr, caliz duhr. Antai yo, antai yo. Yee cohr rie, lisso mee. Yom!"

"Very good," said the eagle. "You're now ready to sing in the night sky. I think you're even ready to fly."

"But, I, I can't fly," Ben stuttered.

"Oh yes you can. How do you think we birds stay in the air? If we had to rely just on our wings alone we wouldn't have a prayer. It's the magic in our song that lifts us up from the Earth's gentle pull, and lets us soar beyond imagination."

Ben protested. "But . . ."

"No buts tonight. You must believe me. Just as you believed the great oak, the falcon, and the light that pierced your heart. It's time to take another chance. We have an important rendezvous with old friends. They're dying to see you again." The eagle chuckled. "Just sing the song and follow me as I fly. Remember, it's the song that lifts you into the sky."

Ben sang out. He felt . . . lighter. "Sah yah harh woo hooo." He lifted off the branch. "Ben lah ho lah doo." Above the tree he soared like a rocket on the fourth of July. "Ahziz ruhr." Off toward the mountains he turned. "Caliz duhr." Higher yet he soared. When he glanced to his left, there was the eagle with his wings stretched wide. "Antai yo, antai yo." His speed became dizzying as he soared back toward earth. "Yee cohr rie," he yelled with fright. Quickly his flight evened out. "Lisso mee." Gently he settled to earth. He was standing in a huge dell. "Yom!"

As far as Ben could tell his feet had touched the ground, yet his heart was still soaring beyond the mountains, beyond the limits of the eye.

Looking around it first seemed as if he were alone. But on the edge of the woods shone small bright lights. There wasn't a sound. Ben turned slowly. The lights surrounded him.

All at once they began to dart back and forth among the trees, whirling. He tried to follow them with his eyes, but his head was spinning. Unexpectedly, they came rushing toward him and splashed all over him, around him, above him, and below him. Now he was inside the light, looking out. Nothing was the same to his eyes. Each tree, each stem, each blade of grass spoke its name. One thing after another introduced itself. Each had a name that seemed as long as a book. It was a feast of words painted like pictures.

"Sedcooworkatochadoo."

"Mollywollotottot."

"Safedobadeebaroo."

"Feeyohumlufoo."

"Ooocacoora."

Shimmering and sparkling, the light splashed from the trees to the grass. Ben swore he could hear songs blowing in the wind. They were the sweetest sounds he had ever heard.

Without his knowing it, the light had lifted him up, gently, just a few feet. As he looked down he saw a sparkle at his toes. The smile on his face seemed to stretch all the way around his head.

As if from nowhere, a large luminous seat moved up from behind him. Gently he was lowered until he sat there supported by nothing but light and air. From the sky came two loud screeches. Swooping down to land in front of him were the eagle and the falcon. They, too, had changed. Their feathers were glistening, and waves of color flowed into the sky each time they moved their wings. Ben sat in wonder.

The eagle spoke. "Our dear Ben, we brought you here this night to initiate you into the magic of light. You see, long ago, the people of Luan lost their sense to see what is aglow. Yet it's not the eyes that see. It's your heart that embraces all that is, and all that can be. The heart is the magic wand and sees both the forest and the trees. It lights up this world with all that can please. This night, we bring you your inner sight. We bring you into the truth of life."

He stepped back. The peregrine falcon stepped forward, bowed his head, glistening with the fire of red.

"Ben, you are so young. Too young, I think, to bear the weight of this world. Yet, for reasons unknown to me, your soul is here to lift us up and reestablish the link that was lost so long ago. Remember, when you're tossed about on the wings of change, when people look aside, thinking you're strange, it is at times like these to think of us. We're not far away. We're as near as the breeze, drifting above looking out for you below." He paused and looked deeply into Ben's eyes. "I beg you, let not the tide carry us all away, to a day with no light."

The falcon then stepped back to join the eagle. Lifting up into the sky they left behind sparks and eddies of swirling fire, and then they were gone.

Ben looked in every direction. All the lights had disappeared! He was sitting in the middle of the dell on an old tree stump! He laughed and smiled, because what he now saw was something even more exciting and thrilling than the giant creatures with trees on their heads. The whole world looked as though it were on fire. Even the gentle wind seemed to fan red flames. Yet nothing burned! Everything glowed bright in the dark, dripping gold.

He closed his eyes, giggled, then laughed, and fell over on his back. Rolling like a log through the long grass, he reached the edge of the woods, sat up, and said, "Where am I?" Makes no difference, he thought. With all the words I've been taught, I can return home with a song and a laugh. I can fly in the air like the eagle and the falcon. I can leave a trail of fire through the skies and all below will think they see meteors. Don't they know that meteors are just a disguise!

He looked down at himself with amazement. From his chest a light was shining, darting about, wrapping around trees and animals in the dark. Ben realized that now he was no longer just a member of the people of Luan. He belonged to the Kingdom of Nowt. Shouting at the top of his lungs, he sang, "Sah yah harh woo hoo!" He lifted up above the dell. In the distance were the lights of his town and the roar of the cars' sound. "Ben lah ho lah do!" Higher yet he soared. With a mighty voice he roared, "Ahziz ruhr, caliz duhr!" In the sky a meteor shower rained down. Never had he seen such a show. Down below, wouldn't you know, everyone looked up, and stared. For a moment, all those people forgot every care and woe.

"Antai yo, antai yo!" Ben circled further into the sky. "Yie cohr rie." He started a swooping descent to the earth. "Lisso mee. Yom!" His feet settled down, but not on the branch of the tree of his father's construction site! Now he stood in his backyard as best as he could see! The heaviness of sleep seemed to fall on him from nowhere. Fighting it off, he made his way up the stairs to his bed. When his head hit the pillow he was fast asleep.

Chapter 9

Imagine his parents' surprise and fright, not to speak of the reporters' excitement, when they saw in the dim morning light that Ben was no longer up in the tree. They looked in every possible place, but he was not to be found.

Where he had been sitting in the tree, there was now an eagle, resting its wings and preening its feathers. His mother's first thought was that the eagle had eaten her little Ben! "Call the sheriff, call the police!" she yelled. "He's been kidnapped. He's lost. I'll do anything, whatever it costs to get my dear Ben back!" She ran from the field back to the construction office.

Ben's dad hesitated to follow her. He stood looking up at that great bird as everyone else scattered and hollered in a panic. When all the people cleared away, he wondered aloud, "Do you know where I can find my Ben?" In his mind came the thought, "Alone, in bed at home. Safe for now, but soon to roam."

He broke into a run and caught up with his wife. "Follow me. Don't ask me why. I think he's home asleep. I'm certain he's fine and safe!" They sped along country roads in a tense silence until they turned into the long drive at their house. Leaping from the car, they ran up the stairs, and stood in the bedroom doorway breathless.

There was Ben asleep, clothes on, filthy, with the cat curled around his collar. Tears rolled down from his parents' eyes. They wondered how in the world he had hidden from them in the night. And how did he make it back home before daybreak?

Slipping into the room, they sat down on the edge of the bed. Ben's dad stroked the hair on his son's head and gave him a gentle shake.

"Ben. Wake up."

Ben opened his eyes. Streaming from each of his parents were fire and light! He had never seen anything so bright. There were trails of wondrous colors, as in the night. He rubbed his eyes, yet they still beamed.

"Am I in trouble?" he asked.

"I don't know what you're in Ben," his father replied. "We'll need to talk about that. For now, we're just happy you're home and safe. I want you to get out of these dirty clothes and bathe. We can talk about this more over breakfast."

Ben nodded, without saying a word. His parents got up and left the room. Sliding from the bed, he peeled off his clothes and went into the bathroom where his mother had started the water running in the tub. As he sat there on the edge of the bath waiting for it to fill, his mind roamed over images of flying with Eagle and the field with all that light.

"Don't let the tub overflow!" his mother yelled up the stairs.

He turned the knobs quickly and the water flowed from a trickle to a drop. He first tested the temperature with one foot, then slid the other beneath the water's surface and wiggled his toes. He sat. Splat went the sound of the tub as tiny tidal waves hit the walls and cracked together in the middle. He laughed.

"Everything all right up there?" his mother yelled.

"Yeah, Mom," he screamed back, giggling to himself.

It wasn't just the splashes that filled him with joy and laughter. It was the sparkles of shimmering silver and gold that cascaded back and forth across the water's rolling surface, at first tumultuous, then softly flowing all around him. Taking a handful, he dripped it over his head, and watched as it rolled sparkling down his nose. When he licked the drops they burst into golden bubbles and floated across the room until they exploded into bright, sunny moons. His merrymaking was interrupted by a knock at the door.

"Ben, breakfast will be ready in ten minutes. Let's get dried and dressed."

"Okay, Mom. I'm coming."

When he climbed into the seat at the breakfast table, both his parents watched him intently.

"Everything all right?" his dad asked.

Ben nodded.

"Do you want grits with your eggs?" his mom asked.

Ben nodded again.

In near silence they ate their breakfast. When Ben finished he put his fork down and sat quietly with his eyes fixed on his lap. He was certain his father was about to mete out some awful punishment. Would they understand why he did what he did? Could he tell them about the eagle, the falcon, and the field of light? His flying through the sky? How could they ever believe that? No one would listen. His stomach began to twist and turn as he fidgeted in his chair. He rocked his feet back and forth, and lightly kicked the leg of the table.

"Ben, could you not do that please?" his dad asked.

"Oh! Sure."

His father took a deep breath. "I don't know where to begin." He tapped his fingers on the table four times. "For starters, I guess I need you to help me understand what that was all about yesterday," he said, folding his hands on the table and leaning forward.

Ben sat, dumbfounded.

"Well?" his father said, impatiently.

Ben slowly chose his words. "Well, it's just that I saw those men pulling the trees up, and I now know that's a sin."

"A sin?" his father asked, as he sat back in his chair.

"Uh, huh. You see it's wrong to kill people, and since the treemungermen are like people, but just bigger, then it's wrong to kill them."

"Who are these treemungermen?"

"Well, they're the creatures that live under the ground, and the trees and bushes are the tops of their heads. I swore to them I'd protect them."

"I see," said his father thoughtfully, once again tapping his fingers on the table. "So, when the man at the construction site asked you to move, you decided the only way you could protect them was to climb the tree?"

"Yeah. That was the only thing I could think to do. He was a lot bigger and stronger than me and I figured the branches weren't strong enough to hold him."

"That was very clever of you."

Ben nodded proudly.

"And, you decided to just stay up there until I gave in and said I wouldn't cut the trees down. Did you ever give any thought to how unsafe that might be?"

"Well," stammered Ben, "Pere said he'd protect me."

"Who's Pere?" his father asked, lifting one eyebrow.

"He's a Peregrine falcon," said Ben, matter of factly.

"Hmm. How did Pere tell you this?"

"He spoke to me. Just like we're talking."

"Ben, don't you think you're a little old to be making up all these things? Falcons don't speak!"

"This one did, Daddy. He even brought me water."

Ben's dad scratched the side of his face, then began chewing on his lip. He glanced over at Ben's mom. She looked blankly at him. Her eyes were brimming with tears.

"When I told you I wouldn't cut down the trees, how come you didn't come out of the tree then?"

"I was going to, but the tree shook and wouldn't let me go. It told me that I should spend the night there."

"The tree told you this?"

"It spoke to me in its language, then mine."

With equal emphasis on every word, his father said, "So that's why you wouldn't come down?"

Ben nodded ever so slightly.

"But you did come down."

"No, first I went up."

"Up?"

"Yeah, the eagle came and taught me how to fly."

"Oh?" Ben's dad flashed back in his mind to that eagle sitting in the tree. Had he not heard what seemed to be a message from the bird. But birds don't talk. How could that be? He could feel his heart racing.

"The eagle gave me the magic words so I could fly, and we left the tree in the middle of the night and went far away to a field that was full of light. I sat on a throne and the eagle and the falcon told me all kinds of wonderful things. And everything sparkled!"

Just then his mother cut in. "That's it. I've had enough! How did you get home this morning?"

Ben got scared. He started to cry.

"How did you get home?" she asked again, now even angrier.

"I, I, I flew home Mommy" stuttered Ben as he began to sob.

"Ben, people don't fly. You came down out of the tree when we were asleep and someone gave you a ride home, right?" She didn't wait for Ben to answer. "You know how we've told you never to get in a car with strangers. Do you have any idea how much I've worried about you? I can't stand that you keep making up these fairy tales and lies. You've got to stop it!" She was practically screaming now, and Ben got more scared and cried even harder.

Ben's father looked at his mother, then at Ben, then back again at his mother. "Ben, I think you ought to go to your room and play. We'll talk more about this later. I need to speak to your mom right now, alone."

Ben pushed back from the table, and with his head hanging low, slowly climbed the stairs. When he got to the top, he plopped down on the landing as he often did when his parents talked in the kitchen. Feeling sad, he wondered how he could prove to his parents that this was all real, and that he wasn't making it up. Downstairs, they were whispering loudly.

They always did this when they didn't want him to hear, but he always could.

"The boy is not well. He's not acting right," his mom was saying. "A child his age should not be talking to birds and making up lies about flying. I'm worried John. We've got to do something."

"I just think it's a phase he's going through."

"Talking to trees and thinking he's a bird is not a phase!"

"I know, I know. But listen, maybe in some way he's just sensitive to nature and . . ."

"Look who's talking. You're the one cutting down the trees."

"Yes, yes, but . . . when I was standing out there under that tree after you went looking for him this morning, I was watching the eagle that had perched right where Ben had been the night before. And I . . . I asked the eagle where Ben was. That's when I got the distinct feeling that he was home, safe. I mean, the bird didn't exactly talk to me. I just got this feeling. I don't know how to describe it."

There was silence for a few moments. Ben strained to hear.

Then his mother said, "John, so you actually believe he can fly?" Ben's dad just stared at the floor. "I'm taking him to Dr. Sanders this morning. I think he's in trouble and needs help, not a parent reinforcing his crazy fantasies." She stormed out of the kitchen into the hallway and saw Ben sitting at the top of the stairs. "Ben, I don't want you to be going far from the house. We're going to go see Dr. Sanders today for a checkup."

Ben nodded, got up, walked into his room, closed the door behind him, and crawled onto the bed face down. Thurston, his cat, was curled in a ball sleeping by the pillow. As he lay his head by Thurston's, Ben began to cry. He had never felt so confused in all his life. "Oh Pere, what am I going to do if no one believes me?" he sobbed.

"It'll be all right. Just hold to the course, and the light will lead you to your source."

Ben looked up to see who had spoken, but there was no one in the room. Just he and Thurston. He crawled from the bed and went to the window. The large oak was silently blowing in the breeze. Shaking his head, he sat back on the bed and scratched Thurston behind the ears. "They think I'm crazy Thurston, but I'm not."

"I know you're not," said Thurston.

Ben stared at him in disbelief. "You talked!"

"Of course. What did you expect?" said Thurston between yawns. "Just because I sleep all the time doesn't mean I'm dumb, you know. In fact, I'm doing important work while I'm sleeping." He licked his right paw, and cleaned his face. Then he reached his left paw out and extended his claws. "By gosh, I haven't been scratching on that post enough. They look a little uneven. What do you think?"

"What difference does it make what I think. Why haven't you ever spoken to me before?"

"Well, I tried speaking to your parents once, but they couldn't hear me. So I figured you couldn't either."

"And you know about the treemungermen, the falcon and eagle, and the lights in the woods . . ."

"I know it all. I'm the scout. I report straight to the Light above, while I'm napping, of course."

"The scout?"

"Yes, that's my job. To keep an eye out, and protect you, too. You don't think I'm just out playing when I'm chasing butterflies? That's all a disguise. I'm here to report on the progress of your education in the earth and the sky. I report to Him on high."

"Who's Him?" asked Ben as he cocked his head.

"You know!"

"No, I don't."

"Now, don't be difficult with me. If it weren't for Him you and I would just be a bubble in his eye. It's He who made us, and He who brought the light. And it's He who gives the birds their flight. Oh, how I love birds!" Thurston smacked his lips.

"Have you ever met Him?" asked Ben.

"Oh, no, no, don't be silly. You don't meet Him like you meet any cat or thing. You . . . sense Him with your . . . whiskers."

"How can you know somebody through your whiskers?"

"How else could I know anything? Why do you suppose that whiskers are so long? And why do you suppose that I have whiskers and you have none?"

"I don't know. I never thought about it. My daddy has whiskers."

"He does not! Those are hairs. Whiskers are very special, my friend. Frankly, I can't for the life of me see why the Light above would have anything to do with you, given that you have no whiskers!" said Thurston with a huff.

"You don't have to get so mad about it," Ben turned his shoulder to Thurston.

"Not mad, just confused. You're the one they think is mad," said Thurston, stretching his paws forward, touching Ben on the hand.

"What do you mean?"

"Hmmm. Frankly, I've never quite understood that myself. But it seems that talking to trees and cats can make one mad in the eyes of the older ones with no whiskers. They can't see beyond their nose, and step only as far as their toes. Most of all, they get scared when they meet someone who knows . . . Him. Beware, they can be unkind, and certainly no friend to one who intends to protect the Kingdom for all time."

"But you still haven't told me who He is."

"Yes, yes. It's just so difficult to talk about. There are so many ways to go. Some things we see and feel, but some things we just know. Take the air, for example. Without it we couldn't live for even a minute. But there is so much air we often forget to thank it for being there, and here, and everywhere. In fact, you never have to worry about the air, except in some places where it's dark and ugly, sick, and dying. Oh, if people could hear the sound of dying air, they surely would stop in their tracks and do something right away to revive it, to make it fresh again."

"That's what Pere said yesterday. We have to be grateful for everything."

"I heartily agree. If you truly see, the world is a magical place. Like the beauty of the sunset. It's a marvel grander than anything a Luanian could make. And since we did not make it, perhaps something much larger did. Something that we call. . . Him! No, Ben, I have never seen Him. But I know that He is there because you can see his footprint in the sky, and his fingerprint on your face."

"I have fingerprints on my face?" Ben rubbed his cheek.

"Yes. I can see them. In fact, I can see his fingerprints better on your face than on all of the others. Mmmmmm. In the last few days everywhere He's touched you is glowing, bright."

Ben looked down at himself. "And He made me like the sunset?"

"Quite definitely!" Thurston nodded.

"And the treemungermen?"

"Most certainly. In your case I think He made you when He made the Treemungermen. You are a very old soul."

"What does that mean?"

"Well, there are some souls who have been here many times before. I suppose He decided it was time for you to return, too. In any event, you have a very special mission I am told. A great deal of work to do." Yawning, he said, "It makes me so tired thinking of it all. You don't mind if I nap here for a few minutes, do you? This business of talking is so much work." Thurston closed his eyes and began to snore.

"Wait. Why did He choose me? And what am I supposed to do?"

Yawning again, Thurston said, "That can all wait for another time. Besides, your mother's getting ready to call for you to go to the doctor."

From the bottom of the stairs, Ben's mom yelled up, "Get your shoes on, Ben. Dr. Sanders said he could see us if we come right now."

"Okay, Mom." Turning to Thurston, he asked, "How did you know that?"

"Oh, silly child, knowing the future is as easy as knowing the past. It's all within your grasp. Now run along." Thurston rolled over on his back and fell fast into a cat nap.

Chapter 10

Ben and his mom rode in the car to Dr. Sanders's office without saying a word. Ben stared out the window as the trees passed by. He didn't want to see the doctor, and even thought of saying the magic words to fly away, but that would upset his mother. So he closed his eyes and kept to himself, to his thoughts and his dreams.

Almost as though it were real, he could see his friend the eagle soaring in the sky, and Pere, the falcon, circling below. There were the treemungermen, dancing around a fire with light streaming from their faces. They were glowing. Maybe Thurston was right. Maybe this was all because of Him.

"Ben. We're here."

Ben opened his eyes and sighed.

"Now listen, the doctor is just going to check you up. No shots. Okay?"

"Okay," he answered meekly.

In the waiting room were two women holding babies. While Ben's mom checked in with the lady at the window, he walked over and stared at one of them. The baby had light glowing all around him, but in some places there were splotches of darkness. "What's wrong with him?" he asked the woman.

"I don't know sweetheart. He just doesn't seem to be feeling very well. I think he has the flu." Ben reached out and touched his head where one of the dark spots was, and it disappeared. Then he touched another one, and the baby giggled. And another one right on his belly and all the dark places suddenly popped and disappeared. The baby started to laugh. Pinkness returned to his cheeks, and his fever evaporated in the air.

"Ben, they're ready for us now," his mother said, and Ben ran to his mother's side. Together they went through the door and down the hall to the examining room.

His mother sat on the metal chair and Ben sat on the big table with paper from one end to the other. Together they fidgeted for a few restless minutes. Then Dr. Sanders came in. He was an old man, nearly seventy, with pink cheeks and a bushy grey moustache. His belly was full and round like his bald head.

"Well, how are you today, Ben?"

"Okay, I guess," he said shyly.

"What's this your mother's telling me about you climbing up trees?"

"It's really no big deal," Ben spoke under his breath while looking at the floor.

The doctor felt Ben's forehead. "That's what I think. Let's just take a look at you here."

Ben started to relax. He liked Dr. Sanders.

"Open your mouth wide now." Ben stretched his mouth as wide as he could. "Thataboy. Hmmm, hm. Looks fine. Now turn your head to the side and let me look into that big ear of yours. Yep, as I suspected, clean as a whistle. Now, Ben, why don't you pull off that shirt and let me give a listen to that ticker." Ben did as he was told. Still on his chest was the mark left by the ball of light that went streaming through his heart. The doctor stepped back to look at it. "Hmm." Then taking the stethoscope he went from one spot on Ben's chest to another, listening carefully. "Yessiree, best heartbeat I've heard today." Then he turned to Ben's mom. "Ellen, you don't mind if Ben and I have a word, man to man, do you?"

"Of course not, Doctor. I . . . I'll just wait for him out in the lounge." His mother got up, but before she left the room, she cast a worried glance back at Ben, then at the doctor.

"Ben, why don't you put your shirt on and sit down over there," he said, pointing to the chair next to the door. Ben hopped down from the table, slipped his shirt over his head, and he and Dr. Sanders sat down across from each other. Dr. Sanders leaned over and placed his elbows on his knees, resting his chin in the palms of his hands.

"Looks like your mom's pretty worried about you, but I don't see a thing wrong. Now, what's all this ruckus you caused down at your dad's construction site? People in town say you're practically a hero for saving all those trees. That was a pretty darned brave thing to do. Tell me, how did you get the great idea?"

Ben wasn't certain he could trust Dr. Sanders. "I don't know. It just wasn't right to have all those trees cut down. I'm not sure why I did it."

"You know, that's exactly what most heroes say. They don't know why they do great things. I think that sometimes we do what just has to be done. Anyway, no matter what your parents think, I think you did a good thing. I wish more people cared like you. Funny, sometimes it takes a child to show us adults what's right."

Ben was warming up to Dr. Sanders. He was the first person who really understood, and cared.

Dr. Sanders continued. "You know, when I was a kid, I sometimes saw funny things. Tried to tell my parents about it, but they thought I had imaginary friends. They didn't want to listen. But I can tell you, it was like magic. Trees would come to life for me. They even spoke. Sometimes at night I'd sneak out and play with them. But one day I went out to play, and they didn't talk back. Thought maybe I'd done something wrong. For the longest time I carried a sadness in my heart. Couldn't tell anybody about it. When I got older, I forgot all about my friends in the woods. But you know, I always believed in them, because one night, while I was out playing, they took me to a field filled with lights. One of those lights went streaming into the sky and came back crashing into my chest. It left a mark on me, just like yours!"

Dr. Sanders unbuttoned the middle buttons on his shirt, and there over his heart was the same mark that Ben had, but fainter. Ben stared wide-eyed. Without even thinking, he reached out and touched it. It glowed. He pulled his shirt up to his neck, and his mark was glowing too. Together, he and Dr. Sanders let out a big laugh.

"So tell me of the Treemungermen! Are they as tall and big as I remember, and do they still carry on with music and dancing until dawn?"

"Yeah! And I get to ride on their shoulders, and the eagle even taught me how to fly."

"You learned how to fly?"

"Sure. All I have to do is say the right words and I'll lift off right into the sky!"

"I'll be. Never had any eagles visit me before. Had a falcon once, but never an eagle."

"A peregrine falcon?"

"You, too?"

"Yeah. He brought me cactus leaves while I was up in the tree."

"Incredible! Tell me, what did he say to you?"

"That the trees and the earth are dying, and if someone doesn't do something quick, there won't be any more treemungermen left in the world. They've asked me to help them."

"Well, that explains a lot of what your mom's been telling me." Dr. Sanders gazed up toward the ceiling of the room for a long time, not saying a word. Then he looked back at Ben. "You know, Ben, I don't think there's a thing you or I could say to make your parents understand this. And I have a feeling you have a calling in this life to do something very special. But how do we handle your mom and dad? That's the question. I tell you what. I think we need to make this a secret between you and me right now. Let me think about it. In the meantime though, just keep it to yourself. Of course, you can call me. And... one other thing Ben. Do you think the treemungermen would allow me to see them again?"

"I dunno."

"It'd do an old guy like me good to sing and dance like I used to. No harm in seeing what they think, huh?"

"Sure, Dr. Sanders, I'll ask them tonight."

"And Ben. Be careful who you tell about this. Most people won't understand. Now get along out to the waiting room and tell your mom I want to speak to her for a moment." He placed his big hand on Ben's shoulder and smiled.

When Ben entered the lounge, his face was beaming. His mother's face, on the other hand, was twisted with worry and concern. But when she saw Ben, even the furrows in her forehead relaxed. "Honey, what did the doctor say?"

"Oh . . . not much. He wants to talk to you."

"Okay. You wait here. I'll be back in a minute."

Ben sat down and swung his legs back and forth, closing his eyes. In his imagination he saw Scrawlyknot. Caught in Scrawlyknot's long beard was a small bird. Its wing seemed to be tangled in the fork of a large root. Scrawlyknot reached out and gently freed it. But it didn't fly away at first. Perching on Scrawlyknot's nose, it began to sing. "De de de de de deeeee de de de de de deeeee." Then Scrawlyknot wiggled his nose and the bird leaped into the air. The giant let out a belly laugh. Ben began to giggle to himself. He loved Scrawlyknot.

"Ben," his mother said, standing in front of him, "What are you laughing at?"

Ben opened his eyes, and every mother and child in the waiting room was staring at him. "Oh, nothing, Mom, just had a funny thought."

"Well come on, we need to be getting home."

On the drive back, his mother seemed much more relaxed. Ben, tired from being up the whole night before, closed his eyes, and was fast asleep by the time she pulled the car out of Dr. Sanders's parking lot onto Ferrell Street. When they got home she lifted his limp body out of the car, carried him upstairs, and tucked him into bed. Ben woke only once, to eat dinner, and went right back to sleep. He didn't wake again until eight o'clock the next morning.

Chapter 11

When Ben opened his eyes, Thurston was sitting on his chest, staring at him. "Ohh. I dreamed a treemungerman was sitting on my chest. What do you want?" said Ben, still in a groggy haze from his long sleep.

"Nothing. Just curious."

"Huh?" he said, still half asleep.

"I heard about the ruckus you created yesterday. That's all your parents talked about through the evening. As soon as I thought they'd said everything that could be said on the subject, they'd say something else. Oh, how humans go on and on about the silliest things!"

"What did they say?" Ben propped himself up on his elbows.

"Nothing that can't wait. To me it was all a bunch of hay. But never mind, we have more important things to speak of today. You and I have an adventure. I'm not to say where, but you're going to love it when we get there."

Ben reached out and scratched Thurston's head, first behind the ears and then under the chin.

"Ooh, I do like that," he said, purring.

"Why can't you tell me where we're going?"

"Because, it's a . . . secret."

Ben stopped scratching.

"Ooh. Don't stop now!" Thurston protested.

"I won't scratch you anymore unless you tell me where."

"Oh . . . all right, scratch my back next."

"Not where to scratch you, silly! Where are we going?"

"I'll tell you," he said sulking, "but only if you scratch my tummy as well." Thurston rolled over on his back and stretched, first one way with his left paw forward, then the other way with his right paw forward. Ben dug his fingernails into his thick fur. "You drive a hard bargain, Ben."

"Well, where?" Ben said, now fully awake.

"If they find out I told you they'll pull out my whiskers one by one," cried Thurston.

Ben gently took hold of one of Thurston's whiskers and gave it a light pull.

"You're as bad as they are! Well, if you must know, we're going to the mouth of the stream. She's so talkative we'll probably be bored to death with all her babbling!"

"That must be really far away."

"It is."

"How are we going to get there and be back before supper?"

"I don't rightly know. I can't have the answer to everything. You're the chosen one anyway. You should be able to figure it out. There must be a way, at least that's what they say. In the lore of the river the way to the mouth is through the mouse."

"The mouse?"

"That's right. And I can't eat it either!" he said with a low growl. "I hate it when they ask such sacrifices of me."

"But where am I to find this mouse?"

"Don't worry about the details. All these things have a way of taking care of themselves. Besides, I'm hungry. A nice, big can of tuna would hit the spot." Thurston rolled over onto the bed, arched his back as he stretched every muscle, and in one motion sprang to the floor and leaped down the stairs.

Ben, too, sat up, and stretched. He was out of his pajamas and into his dungarees and sneakers in less than a minute. He roared down the stairs that led to the kitchen. His mother and dad had just finished eating.

"Good morning, sleepyhead. We began to think you'd never wake up. Hungry?" his mother asked.

"Yeah." Ben climbed up on the seat next to his father.

The morning newspaper was folded next to his empty cereal bowl. On the front page, in big, bold letters it read: Young Boy Saves Trees! Developer Forced By Son To Alter Design. Below it was a picture of Ben on a high limb, and a separate picture of his father down on the ground talking up to him. Ben looked at his dad who had a scowl on his face.

Taking a gulp of coffee first, his father said, "You're quite a hero, young man. Do you have any idea the trouble you've caused me?"

Ben cowered a little. "No."

"Well, you have," he said, letting out a deep sigh. "If you ever disobey me like that again, there are going to be some serious consequences, young man. Do you understand? And another thing, the next time you want to save a tree, promise you'll come to me first."

Ben nodded sheepishly, then looked at his mom.

"Cereal or eggs this morning?"

"Can I have both? I'm really hungry."

His father got up and kissed his mother good-bye, grabbed his briefcase on the counter, and headed out the door.

Ben poured himself some cereal while his mom was busy frying the eggs. He turned back to the newspaper, reading the article as he spooned cereal into his mouth. The story about him went all the way down the side of the front page and continued on page six. He was amazed at all the things they said about him. "Brave." "Wise beyond his years." "Gifted." "A sane voice needed in today's world." "Full of imagination." The list went on and on.

"Wow!" he shouted. "Look at what they said about me."

His mother placed the eggs in front of him, and looked over his shoulder at the article. "Listen, Ben."

He stopped reading and looked up.

"In the eyes of many people, what you did yesterday was a good thing. You're a hero. But not doing what your father told you was not right. You've caused him a lot of trouble, not to speak of the money it's going to cost him. I want you to promise you'll never, ever again do anything like this to hurt us."

Ben kept his eyes on the eggs. "I don't know."

"What do you mean, 'You don't know'?"

"It's just . . . ."

"Just what?"

"I can't say that I won't ever climb up in a tree again to stop people from cutting it down. I made a promise."

"To whom?"

Ben thought about his conversation with Dr. Sanders. He figured he better not say any more right now about the treemungermen. "To myself. That's all Mom. Can we not talk about this anymore?" He picked up his fork and stabbed a big hunk of scrambled egg.

"Just remember what I said." She turned and left the room in a huff.

When Ben was through eating, he went to the bread box and took out four slices and spread them on the counter. Out of the refrigerator he got the peanut butter and grape jelly, and quickly made two sandwiches. He wrapped them tight, grabbed a handful of sunflower seeds from the jar on the counter and stuffed them into his top pocket, ran up to his room, and put the sandwiches neatly into his backpack. Fixing his favorite cap firmly on his head, he ran back down the stairs, and yelled, "I'll be outside in the woods. See you later." He was gone before his mother could protest.

As she watched him run through the yard from her bedroom window, she felt worried, but remembered what Dr. Sanders had said. "Give him some free rein. He's trying to feel his oats as a person. Some kids just need to let their imagination roam."

Ben ran to the edge of the woods and stopped. He didn't even know where he was going! Where was Thurston when he needed him? I'll go to the stream, he thought. Maybe I'll find the little mouse there.

Into the woods he trudged until he came to the edge of the gurgling water and sat down on his favorite boulder. The sun's rays were poking through the canopy of trees overhead. They made an ever-changing pattern on the rock as the wind rustled the leaves.

He thought, now what am I supposed to do?   Closing his eyes, he tried to imagine what the mouse looked like. Suddenly he heard a high pitched voice. "Come, come. We haven't time for the daydreams of fools!" At the same time he felt a tug at the cuff of his dungarees, and opened his eyes in a fright. There, standing on two legs before him, was a mouse, black as coal with a white stripe running from the crown of his head down to his nose.

The little creature snapped, "Now listen young man, I don't know who you are to command so much attention from my brothers the treemungermen, but I don't want you giving me any trouble, do you hear? And another thing, that cat of yours makes my blood boil! If he joins us and raises even one paw in my direction, I'll turn him into scrambled eggs. Understand? And another thing. The last time I had to guide a Luanian, all he did was complain. Not enough food. Not enough light. Not enough air. Always in a fright. You're not going to be like that now, are you?" Before Ben could answer, he continued. "And there are some other rules you must follow if we're going to spend the day together. First, speak when you're spoken to, but don't creak a word, especially if the stream is talking and I'm in the middle of a verb. Second, you must never reveal to the people of Luan the path we take. It's magic. In the wrong hands it can only produce hate. Third, my name is Lorno, but you may call me Lor. And fourth, but most important, don't ever, ever, step on my tail."

Ben had never heard anyone speak so fast. He started giggling uncontrollably.

Lorno pursed his lips. "Are you laughing at me?"

"I guess I am. You talk so fast. My ears could hardly keep up with your mouth. I'm sorry. I didn't mean to make fun of you."

"Apology accepted. You must understand. It's very hard for me to live in a world that goes so slow. I'm impatient, you know." Sticking his nose into the air and sniffing, then looking at the sun, he started grinning. "Time to go! Ho yah hah ho!" He jumped from the rock and ran twenty paces upstream. Turning, he looked back at Ben who had barely moved. "Are you coming? We have no time for anyone who's slow!"

Ben jumped down from the rock where he found Thurston patiently waiting, and set off into the woods practically running to keep Lorno in sight.

"What a snotty fellow," Thurston said. "Did I not tell you that he's an impossible creature? Who could ever have the patience for someone so impolite. I'd rather eat a mouse like that than listen to all his fickle talk."

"Now," said Ben, stopping in his tracks, "promise not to place a paw on Lorno, or else you return to the house!"

"Oh, all right. If you insist. But you're asking an awful lot of a cat, you know. Where is he, anyway?"

Ben looked around for Lorno. He'd been so busy talking to Thurston, he'd lost track of the mouse. "Lor, are you around?" he yelled. There wasn't an answer. "Now you've done it. He's gone!"

"Don't lose faith so quickly! He's just up the way a bit, I'm sure. I'll sniff him out. Wait right here. More importantly, do not fear." Thurston jumped head-on into the brush, and his furry tail disappeared.

Ben quietly waited, looking every which way, but the forest was so thick he couldn't see ten yards in front of him. Where are they? he thought. He waited another few minutes, but still there was no sign of cat or mouse. Maybe I'll just venture into the woods a little farther, and I'm sure I'll find them. He set off in the direction he had last seen Lorno.

"Lorno! Thurston!" he screamed, every few steps. But the only sound was the creaking of the trees as they blew in the wind. "Thurston! Lorno!" Ben was all alone.

To his left he thought he heard something rustling in the brush. "Lorno? Thurston?" There was no reply.

To his right he heard something rustling. He turned quickly, but couldn't see a thing. "Lor. It's me, Ben."

The trees continued to bend and creak, and his loneliness grew. Following the path of the stream, he moved forward, but now the brush was getting thicker, and it was becoming more and more difficult to make his way.

"Ow!" he screamed, as a branch scratched him across the cheek. He reached up to feel the wound. When he pulled his hand away it was smeared with blood. Stooping at the stream he washed his face and winced at the sting. Tears streamed down his cheeks. How am I going to find the mouth of the babbling brook? he thought. I'm lost. "Thurston. Lorno. Where are you?"

"Don't worry, you have set the right course."

Ben turned quickly. There was no one around. "Who's there?" he asked, frightened.

"I am," came a whispered reply.

"Where are you? I can't see you."

"Ah, but you can feel me."

"Feel you?"

"On your cheek. On your hand. I'm beside you as you stand."

Ben touched his cheek with his moist hand and could feel the cool touch of the water. He looked down at the brook as it gurgled past. "Wow, you can talk!"

"I most certainly can. You have come the right way, so do not cry. That wound will heal by and by. Follow me as far as you can, then lie on the sand. In a dream you'll find the source. The truth is waiting for you in due course."

"But . . . what about Lorno, and Thurston? Should I wait for them?"

"Never wait to begin, or else your world will come to an end."

Ben got up and looked around. Slowly he made his way through the brush, this time more carefully. Still it clung to him, reaching out and scratching his arms and face. But he didn't mind now.

Onward he went as the sun rose overhead. The brush got thicker. The trees grew taller. Never before had he been this deep in the woods. There were no signs of people. No sounds of traffic. And if there were planes in the sky, he couldn't see them, because the top of the forest was so thick it was like a tent.

He walked for what seemed to be hours, and was hungry. There, just ahead, was a clearing by the stream. He hurried on. Within just a few moments he was standing on a thin strip of sandy beach.

Sitting down underneath a large spruce tree, he pulled his backpack off and opened the first peanut butter and jelly sandwich. It tasted good. After five bites it was gone. He tore open the wrapper of the second sandwich and finished it off as quickly as the first. Kneeling at the stream, he cupped his hands and brought water to his mouth to drink. He reached down again and splashed his face. When he took his hands away they were sparkling like that night when light shone from every living thing. He smiled. Maybe I'll just rest here for a couple of minutes, he thought. Returning to the large spruce, he sat down, stretched out his legs, and closed his eyes. I wonder where Lor and Thurston are? He yawned, and in a moment drifted off to sleep.

In a dream he saw himself by a stream. He was sleeping with his head resting on his chest. High above him a large eagle drifted in and out of the clouds. Oh, he dreamed, wouldn't it be wonderful to fly that high? At that very instant he left the ground and started to rise, beyond the tops of trees, drifting whichever way he pleased.

Speaking to no one in particular, he said, "I wonder where that silly cat and mouse could be. They left me all alone down there to fend for myself. Oh, who cares. I'm above that now. I think I'll fly over and say hello to my friend in the sky." With the ease of a bird, Ben turned and shot through the air like an arrow. He swerved and tumbled, giggling with delight as the sun caught his eye.

Emerging from a fluffy cloud, Ben rode the air stream next to the great eagle. He could feel the flap of the bird's wings. Rolling over on his back, he glided effortlessly through the air.

The eagle spoke. "So Ben. You're lost. You've wandered in the woods and let your guides get ahead of you. Such a mistake could cost you someday. But this fine afternoon it's a lesson with a small price."

"Do I have far to go?"

"You're as near as your heart and as far as the eye can dart. Wherever they lead, you will follow in tow. Do not look for answers, though. Let your mind sow its seeds, sprouting new thoughts and deeds."

Resting on his elbow high in the sky, Ben listened closely to every word.

Suddenly, he felt a tug from down below. Gravity was pulling him to the ground, and the stream, which seemed so small from high above in the clouds, was growing in size. Quickly descending, Ben returned to the ground and awoke to the strangest sound.

It went crack. He opened his eyes and looked around. There was no one to be found. There it was again. Crack. Crack. Crack! Ben looked down and saw Lorno resting in his top pocket, chomping on sunflower seeds and spitting out the shells.

Lor looked up and paused. "It's about time you returned! I waited and I waited and I waited. But you were flying about with that dreaded eagle, no doubt! He's a nasty fellow when he wants to be. Even if he's wise I don't trust him. But I take my orders, and I don't question one of his feathers when he appears. Oh, excuse me for a second." Crack went another seed. The little mouse nibbled, nibbled, nibbled, licked his paws, then shook from the tip of his tail to the end of his nose. "I do like a good shake. You should try it sometime. But not right now, especially with me in your pocket. Besides, the stream is waiting you know, and the day is growing old. How is it you Luanians can sleep without even letting out a peep?" Leaping from Ben's pocket, Lor scurried ahead into the clearing, and turned. "Are you coming or not, you lazy lout!"

During Lor's longwinded speech Ben sat quietly, perplexed. He couldn't think of a thing to say. Finally he found his tongue. "But what about Thurston?"

"Thurston? That no good cat. A blight on civilization if you ask me. They should all be made into fur caps!"

"Don't you say things like that!" Ben walked over to the mouse, reached down and grabbed him by the tail.

"You let me down, you hear. If you don't let me down right now I'll make my complaints all the way to the One who wears the crown."

"Just hold your horses, my little friend. You've been ugly from the first thing this morning, to me and my cat. I won't stand for it. There's no need for bitter words anywhere in the Kingdom. I don't want to hear your complaints!" Ben brought Lor close to his face, and they were eye-to-eye.

Lor broke his gaze and looked to the ground. He started to weep. Oh, what a mournful sound. Tears streamed down his chin and sprinkled Ben's shin with a tiny shower.

"Why are you crying? I didn't mean to hurt your feelings."

"It's not you. I'm sorry for what I do. I've just run scared all my life. I don't know what it would be like to not argue and complain."

Lor wailed. Ben pulled from his pocket a red bandana and handed it to the mouse. With one big breath he blew his nose, then quickly recomposed himself.

"You have my promise from here on out. I will treat your cat with respect, or at the very least only a little contempt, if you please. You must realize I'm still a mouse and it is so very hard to douse my ways, especially since they've been there from the very first days. Please put me down, we have a long journey ahead, and I'm still not even half-fed."

Ben gently lowered him to the ground. "I like you, Lor of the woods, especially now."

The mouse stood tall, and pulled back a tuft of hair from his eyes. "Follow me to the edge of the stream. There we will find a seam in the earth. Down long steps you'll descend. I can only take you part of the way, but if you tend to the path without delay, the mouth of the stream will greet you surely by the end of the day."

"You're only going part of the way? But how will we get out and home again? And how will we see down there? And what if I get scared? I am already scared. Lor, you can't leave us all alone!"

Lor turned and scurried up Ben's pants leg, along the front of his shirt and sat on his shoulder. "Now, now. We mustn't be frightened of what could be or what we can't see. You must skip from moment to moment like jumping from one rock to another in the stream. Don't pay attention to all those voices of in your head when fear fills your heart. Let your feet make every step a new start. Your path has already been worn by the footsteps of the One. He will be your guide into the great divide. Leading the way is a fire as bright as day. It will singe the darkness and keep it away."

As Lor spoke Ben closed his eyes and sank into the depths of his breath. When he blinked them open, his heart was calm, and he trusted Lor's promise that there was nothing to fear.

Lor searched Ben's face. Satisfied that his words had reached their mark, he scurried down his leg and up the path. "Follow me. Quick now. We have no time to waste. We must find the seam in the earth's red clay. Hurry, hurry!"

Ben ran to keep up with Lorno. Unexpectedly, Thurston joined them along the path. They came to the stream's edge. Lor stopped, sniffed the air while standing on his hind legs, looked upstream, then downstream. "This way, but quietly."

Along the bank they walked. Ben turned and looked behind him. Funny, he thought, our feet aren't leaving footprints in the muddy sand. "Lor," he whispered.

"Shhh!" Lor turned, holding one of his three fingers to his mouth.

"Our footsteps disappear after we step on the sand." Ben whispered as softly as he could.

"This is a magic shore. There has never been a Luanian here before. It sweeps away the footprints so that no one may ever trace our steps to the door. Now, no more talking. We're very near. Keep close by me, and remember, do not fear."

Slowly they crept. With every step Ben thought he could hear unusual sounds. And it seemed as though the trees were turning the colors of fall. They shimmered, bright and iridescent, and as they shook in the breeze, Ben swore he could hear the sound of bells ringing and someone singing a sweet tune.

"Bling dling, bling dling, bling dling. Oh bring us the one who sings. Bling dling, bling dling, bling dling. Oh bring us the one who sings."

"Lor, can you hear that?"

"Shh. What?"

"The trees are singing?"

"Oh, that. They are very pleased with your visit. But remember, you must not tell of this place, or it may be forever lost without a trace. Now, no more talking. Let your ears, eyes, and heart drink in the wonder of this wood. Remember it well, for it is here where you once stood. They are singing to remind you that this world is good."

Ben pondered Lor's words. What did he mean? Nothing in this world was what it seemed.

Lor snapped his fingers then pointed at the ground, chanting, "Sho row, sho row. He no ho lo. It is time to travel into the earth."

At Lor's command, the ground split open nearly five feet wide without a sound. A warm glow poured from the hole, and steamy air blew into their faces. Ben, Thurston, and Lor inched forward and stretched their heads out over the edge.

Thurston, who had been quiet 'till now, spoke first. "If you don't mind, Ben, I think I have some things back at the house to tend. Holes in the ground are not my thing, you know. I'm just a messenger anyhow."

Ben shot back, "Are you chickening out on me now that I need you. Besides, you're my scout forever, and that means today as well. You got me into this, so you have no choice."

Thurston sat back on his hind legs. "All right. If you insist. I'll accompany you. But remember, this is your journey. You take the first step."

Lorno tugged on Ben's pants leg. "The stream and her friends are near. They await you below, so don't fear. One step at a time will be just fine. Don't forget what I told you about jumping from rock to rock. Keep your mind focused as though this were a dream. Do not look back or forward. Do not wander with your eyes or think of anything horrid."

Ben listened to Lor's hasty advice as though he were hearing the words with dream ears. He stepped forward. The light flowing from the hole was almost blinding. Yet it didn't hurt his eyes. His feet guided his way. Into the earth he descended.

Thurston cautiously followed close behind. Within a minute, they had disappeared. As quickly as it had opened, the seam shut, leaving no trace of where they had gone. Lorno turned and ran quickly along the path back into the woods. He had fulfilled his mission, and was eager to return to the ways of a field mouse.

Chapter 12

At first Ben and Thurston could not see where they were going. Yet the ground seemed to come up to meet Ben's every step. The air was musty, rich with the smell of the earth. A constant breeze blew in their face. Faintly, at first, they heard voices ahead of them. As they moved forward, the sounds became louder and more distinct. It was as though the breeze and the noise were the same.

Ben stopped. Thurston stopped, his legs shaking. Turning to look behind him, all Ben could see was darkness.

Thurston hissed, "Where did the hole go?"

"I don't know," Ben replied through his teeth.

"You're sure this place is safe?" Thurston's ears lay back on his head, and the hair on his tail stood straight out.

"Would you like me to hold you?" Ben said, as he bent down to run his hand along Thurston's back.

"That would be nice. I'm chilled and my blood feels like ice."

Ben pulled Thurston to his chest and gently scratched the top of his head and neck. Kissing his ear, he said, "Don't worry. I think we're here for a lesson. There's nothing to fear. Hold tight and I'll carry you the rest of the way."

Ben forged ahead. At every step the air smelled less and less of the earth and more like fresh rain on a cool, spring afternoon. The farther he went, the wider his grin grew. It was like coming home after a long trip. This place under the ground felt familiar, like an old friend.

The corridor widened. Sounds of dripping water and singing rose from below. Glistening, the surface of the walls looked as though they were covered with diamond dust. White, red, purple, green, and yellow light streamed from below. It was as if they had reached the end of the rainbow.

On and on Ben walked with Thurston perched with his two paws over his shoulder. It seemed as though the path had no end. Then, turning a corner, they were dazzled. Sitting on large rocks were creatures made of stone that looked as soft as cotton balls.

Slowly, deliberately they spoke. "What has taken you so long?"

Ben stopped in his tracks. Thurston clung to Ben's shirt, claws outstretched. Large bubbles with pictures spinning on their surfaces popped from the creatures' mouths and floated into the air. They were huge spheres! Bigger than trees. And they were headed right toward Ben and Thurston.

Frightened, Thurston leaped from Ben's arms and scurried up the path. Ben hardly noticed. His attention was focused on the giant bubbles coming his way. Each seemed like a world unto itself. Images of all kinds of things dissolved only to be replaced by new pictures. These were no ordinary bubbles. And the pictures were not like any pictures he had ever seen before. They were more like dreams. Where there should have been sky there was the earth. Rivers flowed up and around the legs of animals, then back into the ground without a sound. Trees grew with their roots sticking straight up. People walked by bouncing on their head. Cats had tails growing out of their ears. Birds flew by tumbling through the air. Buildings walked about on hundreds of legs like centipedes, stepping on anything, without a care. Butterflies bigger than airplanes rested on a single blade of grass.

Ben didn't budge. The thought of running never entered his mind when the first bubble floated right up to his nose. Reaching out his hand, he took a step forward. Suddenly, half of him was in the bubble while the other half stuck out! He took a deep breath. The air was clean and clear. Without another thought, he took a second step and found himself in a magical world.

At first his eyes could not adjust. Swirls of what looked like smoke whirled by his face until they reached the inner surface of the bubble. They thickened and became strange pictures, just like the ones he had seen moments ago. Then they moved and changed, disappearing into the air without a trace. As soon as they were gone, new washes of color swirled by and replaced them. It was like being on the other side of a dream.

What looked like a foamy liquid floated by, almost like air bubbles in the water. They burst above his head letting out all kinds of miraculous sounds. The tinkling of bells, the whooshing of roaring rivers, the breeze rattling trees on a fall day, and the calls of a hundred different wild birds.

There were also tiny whirlwinds spinning all around him, evaporating into the air. When they did, the most luscious smells in the world wafted Ben's way. Pine, spruce, and sycamore. The sweet scent of carnations and magnolias. And the deep, rich aroma of the earth.

His eyes and ears feasted on a thousand sights and sounds, and his nose was transported to new worlds by bouquets of incense that kept rising up from nowhere.

Ben looked down at his feet, but they weren't resting on anything. Yet he was standing as though he were on the ground. Below and above him all he could see was the bubble. Beyond the bubble there was only darkness. He moved closer to the inside surface of the bubble, but could see no traces of the cave where he had just stood moments before! He touched the inside face of the bubble. His hand slipped right through, but he couldn't see it on the other side. Afraid, he pulled his hand back and looked at it. It was whole just like a second before, but it tingled a little. He tried it again, this time sticking his arm out all the way to the elbow. Then he pulled it back. It tingled even more. He tried the other arm. Then both arms together. Each time he stuck them outside the bubble, they disappeared. Each time he pulled them back inside, they reappeared. He loved this magic, and would have continued for some time if he hadn't heard the voice.

"Ben. We didn't bring you here to play all day. As much as you're enjoying the magic of the fentubbles, it's time that we had a discussion about the earth's troubles."

Ben spun around and looked, but could see no one. He half whispered, "Who's there?"

Whatever it was chuckled. "Nothing but the thin air. Out of me comes all that is fair."

"But where are you?" Ben looked above and below and all around.

"Everywhere that you hear my sound."

"How come I can't see you?"

"I am not a thing for the eyes! I live in the world of sound and breath. I travel beyond the currents of time and death. I'm a dream on the tip of your tongue, all the tasks that are undone. I cling close to the earth, and gather my strength and courage from people's mirth. I'm a mystery, yet I'm like a bright, sunny day. Your eyes cannot see me, just like your mind cannot grasp all that will truly last. I cast a shadow on every living thing. Yet when you search for me, I disappear like your hand outside the fentubble. But be certain I am there. I am the air."

"What, what do you want from me?" Ben stammered, as his head sank down into his shoulders.

"It's not what I want, it's what I choose to give. I am here to teach you how to truly live."

"But, I am alive."

"Yes and no. Your breath still has a long way to go."

"I don't get it."

"Without breath there can be no life, and all that's left is a struggle and strife."

"I still don't understand."

"Understanding is for the older ones. It is for those who've stopped breathing and believing. I am here to teach you that the world is not always as it seems. What your parents call the world is more like a dream. Here, this fentubble of air is all that truly is, all that can be. Right here is the beginning of the world and all that you normally see. Deep within, like bubbles bursting on the water's surface, the world is created. All is free here. Nothing is set. The swirl of the air can even free those who fret. Do you not feel free of all trouble here in the fentubble?"

"I guess so." Ben giggled and took a deep breath. As he inhaled he could feel the air stream down to his toes, to the tips of his fingers, then back out through his nose.

"That's exactly what I was hoping to see. A breath as deep as the ocean bed, reaching from your toes to your head. When you breathe like that, you can leave behind the world of the dead."

Ben took another deep breath and felt like a waterfall was cascading through his arms. He jumped and flipped three times in the air. The deeper he breathed, the higher he jumped. He bounced off the top, the bottom, and the sides of the fentubble as though it were a trampoline

"That's it! This feeling will be with you forever and a night. Whenever you choose you may return to the fentubble's inner light. It will help you on your journey to set the world right. Now, I must go. We will meet again."

Ben closed his eyes. He felt as though he were floating. It almost seemed like his head lifted from his body and rose into the light air. Right through the roof of the cave he went, through yards and yards of earth, into the light of day, and higher yet. Onward into the sky he rose, beyond the birds gliding about, past the clouds and satellites whirling at incredible speeds around the earth. He left behind the moon and moved on into the vastness of space. There were stars everywhere, dancing and glittering. Ben's smile kept growing wider and wider. Songs floated by. They rang out like chimes and bells, each note sweeter than the one before.

Ben's head began to spin slowly. He surveyed the universe from all sides. Faster and faster his head spun. Faster and faster the stars careened around him. Soon they were just blurs of light. Still faster he went. No longer could he see the darkness of space. Now everything looked soft and white. Ben let out a scream of glee. Then, like in a dream, it all faded to black.

When Ben opened his eyes he was lying at the stream's edge. Gone were the fentubbles, the cave, the voice of the air. For the longest time he just lay there with his ear against the ground. He stretched his hand out into the cool water. Once again, he closed his eyes. His mind was blank.

When he opened his eyes, Lor, his little mouse friend, was sitting nose-to-nose with him, staring intently. "Well?" Lor asked, his eyes large.

"Well what?"

"You know. Did you see her? Did you talk to the stream? What did you find out? Most important of all, what can you tell me? I want to know everything!"

"My, you certainly are nosey! Why should I tell you a thing after you ran away from me and Thurston at the mouth of the cave. By the way, have you seen Thurston?"

"That no-good cat? I saw him scit-scatterin' home with his tail between his legs. He didn't even have the manners to stop and tell me what happened. Don't you worry about him. He's probably curled up right now in the shade of the old oak tree. So, what was it like?"

"I thought you knew all about these things."

Stammering, Lor replied, "Well, well, of, of course. It's just, just . . ."

"Just that you never have seen the mouth of the stream or know anything about the light of air or dreams. Am I right?"

"So what if I don't know any of these things! I'm only the guide. But I am curious. Was it as magnificent as they say?"

"Yes! But more so." Ben now propped himself up on his elbows.

"Tell me, tell me. I want all the details. Don't dare leave a thing out. What was the cave like? Was it dark? Was it light? You didn't happen to see a nice stash of seeds down there did you? Details! Details! What did it smell like? How many breaths did you take?"

The questioning went on and on. Ben did his best to answer Lor, but every answer brought more questions. Lor's curiosity could not be satisfied. They would have sat there on the banks of the stream for days if Ben hadn't noticed that the sun had disappeared, and it was getting dark.

"Oh my," he said. "It's late. If I don't get home soon, I'm going to be in real trouble. Hurry Lor! Show me the way. I've got to go!" Ben stood, brushed himself off, and headed into the forest. Lor didn't budge. When Ben looked back he saw him still sitting there. "Are you coming?"

"Where?" "To show me the way home. What did you think?"

"The way home? That's a tricky matter."

"What do you mean? It's this way, isn't it?"

"That's what you'd think, because we came from that way, right?"

"Yeah."

"Didn't they teach you anything?"

Ben now retraced his steps to the mouse, and stood towering over him. "Why are you being so stubborn?"

"Me, stubborn? It's you who's being stubborn. If you'd only listen for a moment you'd realize that the way home is not that way," he said, pointing downstream. "It's this way." Lor pointed in the opposite direction.

Ben shook his head. "You don't make any sense."

"Exactly. It makes no sense to go back the way you've come from because by now it's all changed. Besides, it's always much more fun to go back a different way from how you came. That makes it more of a game."

"My parents won't think it's a game if I don't get home soon."

"Well, if it's soon you want, then the path you chose is closed. It's this way that will get you there before the light of the next day." Once again he pointed in the opposite direction.

"You speak in gibberish. I don't think you really know. I'm going this way." Ben headed off downstream.

Lor called after him. "Don't say I didn't warn you!"

Ben didn't look back and picked up the pace, more determined than ever to get home as soon as he could. Before long, though, it became dark and the clouds blocked the light of the moon. Ben lost track of the stream and the path. With every step he became less and less certain of where he was. Within an hour he was hopelessly lost.

In the dimness of the dark night he spied a large outcropping of boulders ahead on the trail. He climbed to the top and stood, turning all the way around, looking for a trail. After completing a turn, he was no closer to knowing where he was than before he climbed the rocks. He shouted. "Lor! Thurston!" All he heard was the stillness of the night air. Again he yelled. "Lor! Thurston!"

In the distance he heard the call of a night owl, "Whoo, whoo, whoo, whoo." Besides the wind, nothing else disturbed the deep, dark quiet that hung like a blanket over the woods.

"Mom! Dad!" he screamed. Little did he know that far away, out of the range of his voice, his parents were also calling him.

Ben sat down on the large rock, all alone. Now he was afraid. It was growing cooler and the chill of the night sent a shiver down his spine. Suddenly, he heard something.

Wheeling about quickly in the opposite direction, he listened closely. He could have sworn he heard a voice. Then he heard it again, but this time coming from the opposite direction. He turned quickly and strained his eyes to see into the darkness.

Hesitantly, he said, "Hello."

There was no reply. Ben took a deep breath, and thought, relax, I'm the protector of the forest. I've got nothing to fear.

He heard the voice again, but this time he didn't turn. He closed his eyes and waited, thinking all the while of those thin bubbles of air and images of the night, goblins, and dragons rising up, only to disappear into a puff of smoke.

Once again, he heard the sound, but this time closer. Still, he did not move. He remembered what the air had said about breathing, and he quietly inhaled, then exhaled, alert.

Whatever it was let out another sound, like a low growl, first to his left, then to his right. Patiently Ben sat still.

Then, as near as an arm's reach, Ben could feel something near. Every time it exhaled it let out a raspy, tinny sound. Still, he did not move. With his eyes closed, he spoke, "Where are you from, my little friend? Where do you heal when you are on the mend? If you come to harm me, then your life is in danger. If you come as a friend, then you must be he whom they call the Ranger. Welcome, Hosoofang."

Ben opened his eyes and slowly turned his head. Sitting on its haunches was a coyote, its eyes shining like two bright stars in the night. Its tongue was hanging out of the side of its mouth. Its nose was as black as coal. It spoke with an old voice that crackled. "You are wiser than I expected. To know a thing's name before ever seeing it requires a heart that can touch the air, a mind that can dream what is not there, a soul that can hold the stars in the heavens like a grain of sand in the hand. Your roots reach deep, Ben of Luan. It's good to see how unshakable you are. You have grown so much in these last few days. It is time to reach your roots into the soil and feel the earth's pulse as though it were your own. Prepare to rejoin the Kingdom, to give your heart the room to know all things small and low, all things that are tall, and must one day fall. As it was written so long ago, people will sit at your feet and rest in your shade to feel life's beat."

Ben reached out and ran his hand across Hosoofang's head, and the coyote leaned into the caress. "What do you mean that people will sit at my feet and rest in my shade? I'm so small I hardly cast a shadow."

"Ah, your shadow will grow in due time. One day it will stretch so far that it will require a year's journey on foot just to reach its end. And the traveler will find himself back where he had begun, at the base of the tree, protected from His sun."

"You talk in riddles that sound like they make sense, but . . ."

"Don't worry. What is a riddle today will be as clear tomorrow as a cloudless night with a full moon. But it's getting late, and your parents are calling you. What is needed now is a quick route home, a path that is clear and straight. A route on which you can make haste."

"I tried every path, but I seemed to keep going in circles."

"That's because I tied the paths into a knot. I didn't want you to leave the forest without knowing you as a little boy, for in the future I will only know you as a treemungerman. But now that we've had our chat, I've untied the paths, just like that." Hosoofang waved his paw through the air. Suddenly, a path as straight as an endless road opened up through the trees, and the moon broke through the clouds, casting a beam of light there on the rock where Ben and Hosoofang sat. "Go now, and do not worry your parents anymore. They'll have plenty to worry about in the days ahead. I'll be back. I have much to say, even in the light of day. Hurry now, before the storm rages. The way through the sage cannot stay open for ever and a day."

Ben reached out and stroked the coyote's nose one last time. Sliding from the rock he ran to the path and turned to say goodbye, but Hosoofang was gone.

The path was straight. Ben ran at full speed. After a few minutes he stopped to catch his breath. The whole sky lit up with a flash. Then the crashing sound of thunder rocked and scared him. Large drops of rain the size of tomatoes began to pummel him. Without warning they turned to hail. The path disappeared and the trees moved in close to protect him. The wind was so fierce that he was battered from every side by the sting of the falling ice. He knelt and held his hands above his head and his arms in front of his face for protection. The hail bruised and cut him.

Almost as quickly as it started, it ended. Ben sat holding himself like a little ball sobbing from the pain. The blood from his wounds ran down his arms and across his face, mixing with rain that now began to fall, staining his shirt.

Ben stood and looked up into the sky, letting his arms drop to his side. The cool rain felt good, and relieved the sting from his hands, arms, and face. He looked around for the path. It was gone. Where there had been a wide avenue was now a thicket of trees and brush. Closing his eyes, he imagined his house, and his parents standing in the rain, calling his name. He turned in a circle until he felt a strange tug at his chest. He somehow knew that was the right direction. With his eyes fixed on a point as far as he could see, Ben moved through the forest quickly. After many minutes of walking, he stopped. In the distance he could hear his name being called. He quickened his pace.

When he emerged from the woods he could see his house. His father was standing in the rain soaking wet and screaming his name. Ben yelled, "I'm here, Dad!"

His father turned and ran toward him. Ben stood still. His head felt dizzy and everything began to spin faster and faster. His father caught him just before he collapsed to the ground.

Chapter 13

When Ben woke, he was tucked neatly into his bed, surrounded by his favorite pillows and stuffed animals, with Thurston sitting on his chest. From the stairwell landing below he could hear Dr. Sanders's voice. Closing his eyes, he strained to hear every word.

"Just keep daubing a little of this lotion on those wounds every two hours or so, and be sure he drinks plenty of liquids throughout the day. Give me a call this afternoon and let me know how he's doing. I'll come around after dinner to check on him."

Ben heard his parents thanking Dr. Sanders. Then the back door slammed. Ben slipped from his bed and went to the window. Down below Dr. Sanders walked to the foot of Scrawlyknot and looked up. Ben saw him say something. The doctor patted the tree on the trunk and turned to walk to his car. Scrawlyknot bent at the trunk, and with one of his branches reached down and knocked the hat right off Dr. Sanders head!

Dr. Sanders let out a huge belly laugh as he picked up his hat. Still laughing and shaking his head, he continued to the car. Ben had never seen Scrawlyknot move in the light of day.

Ben's mom and dad, both watching from the living room window, were spellbound by what they saw! After the doctor pulled out of the driveway, they turned and stared at each other. The blood had drained out of their faces.

"Did you see what I saw?" his father muttered.

His mother nodded, and swallowed.

They turned, without saying a word, walked over and slumped into the couch. His father cleared his throat. "There must be a logical explanation. I mean, trees don't just do that sort of thing. Do they?"

"John, I don't feel well. I think I'm going to be sick." She leaped up and ran to the hall bathroom, slamming the door quickly behind her.

His father followed her to the door. "You all right, honey?" After a few moments he heard a muffled, "Yes." He cracked the door and found her sitting on the edge of the tub. A little color had returned to her face. He took a wash cloth, wet it, and gently wiped her forehead.

While he daubed her face, she said, "I don't know what's going on with Ben. I'm worried. I feel like I'm losing my baby to . . . trees that act like humans. We need to move into town and get away from these woods or something terrible is going to happen. I can feel it. We'll call Jane Madsen today and list the house. And I'll get the movers here by tomorrow, and we can rent an apartment until we find something." She looked up at her husband with sheepish eyes that were now filling with tears. "Am I acting crazy?"

"Naw, you're just upset. Come on in the kitchen and I'll fix you a cup of tea." As they walked down the hall he put his arm around her, stopped and turned to face her. "I don't know any more than you do about what's going on, or if Ben's in any danger. Maybe this is a good thing. Whatever it is, let's just take it a day at a time, okay? And not be too quick to jump to conclusions?" She nodded, he kissed her cheek, and they continued into the kitchen.

As Ben stood at the window watching Scrawlyknot play with Dr. Sanders, he giggled. Quietly, he lifted the window, and whispered, "Scrawlyknot, how come you don't play with me during the day like that?"

The big trunk of the tree slowly bent toward the house, and a branch reached out and touched Ben on the cheek. His cheek tingled! Like magic, all the scratches and bruises disappeared. All the soreness and exhaustion was replaced by a surge of good feelings and energy unlike anything he had ever felt before. Then a strange sensation started to fill his toes and tickle the bottom of his feet. It was like heat, but it didn't burn. The more Ben wiggled his toes the hotter it got.

"Scrawlyknot, my feet feel … well, they feel, weird. What's going on?"

"Shh," came a whispering sound. "Change burns the old to pave the way for the new. Roots can't just grow overnight in the dew. It takes a lot to revive the likes of you, my little treemungerman."

"What do you mean by roots? Am I growing roots?"

"Why of course. How else could you join us in the dark of night as the years pass by? How else could you ever reach so high into the sky? To grow, part of you must die."

"But I don't want to die!"

"Do questions of death muddle your mind? Let me clarify the matter for the last time. Death is a funny thing. It worries many people and treemungermen alike. But those who understand it sing with delight. Before you people of Luan are born, do you really think there's nothing in the horn? There's a whole life before that first cry. There's a soul that knows what it means to be whole. We come. We go. We change. We grow. But what's inside is beyond pain and joy, beyond even what we sow. What we see can fool many of us for a while. We think life is in the beginning and death is in the end. In truth, what you call death is like the wind. What I call life reaches from here to there, a step on the stairs beyond all care. Life does not begin at birth and end at death. Life fills us with breath. It's a miracle to pass this way for even a day, but know there are many other places in which to play. Each is as close to that land where life is always at hand. I assure you, all is just a step along the way for a new leaf sprouts every day. There are many changes waiting for you. Accept them as all part of the plan. Do not try to alter the actions of His hand. With all that is in store, realize that the thing you call death is truly not behind any door. When roots burn from your feet into the ground, rejoice, for the Kingdom of Nowt is about to rebound. At last the people of Luan will sing for love, for life, and for the end of strife."

A voice came up from the stairs below. "Ben? Who are you talking to?"

Ben was startled and turned from the window. "Nobody! Just, myself."

"You're not out of bed now? The doctor said you need to rest and conserve your energy." Ben ran and jumped back into bed.

"Yeah, Mom. I'm still in bed."

"I fixed you some lunch and I'll be up in a minute."

Scrawlyknot had returned to his place in the yard, erect, quietly blowing in the breeze. The burning sensation in Ben's feet had disappeared, at least for now.

When Ben's mom entered the room with a large bowl of vegetable soup and an egg salad sandwich, she stopped two steps from the bed and stared at Ben. "What happened to your face?"

Ben reached up and touched his cheek. "What do you mean?"

"All your cuts and scratches are gone!"

"Oh, yeah."

She set the tray of food down on his desk and sat down on the edge of the bed, running her hand lightly across his cheek. Her mouth hung open in disbelief. She yelled down the stairs. "John! John!"

"Yes, honey," came his father's voice from the kitchen.

"Come up here. I want you to see something."

"On my way."

When his dad sat down on the bed, he looked closely at Ben's face, and also reached out and ran his hand across it. "I'll be!"

"That's all you have to say? 'I'll be.'"

"Well, I've never seen anything heal like this before."

While they talked, Ben sat motionless. He thought, what am I going to tell them? They'll never believe that Scrawlyknot did this. And what are they going to say about the roots that are supposed to be growing from my feet?

"Honey, do you think we should call the doctor again?"

117

"I don't know," his father replied. They continued to discuss Ben's miracle cure, talking about him almost as though he were someplace far away.

At last, his dad turned to Ben. "You had some pretty nasty scratches on your face this morning. Do you have any idea how they could heal so fast?"

Ben shook his head, closely watching their reactions.

"Now Ben," his father coaxed, "these things just don't disappear all by themselves. Is there something you're not telling us?"

Ben pursed his lips, and lifted his eyebrows. Once again he shook his head, but with less conviction.

His mother cut in. "Ben, we need to know." With hesitation in her voice, she said, "Was it your friends from Nowt?"

Ben tentatively nodded. His mom looked to his father, searching his face for what to say or do next. His father, confused as she was, returned her stare. Ben looked from one to the other. Finally, his father sighed and spoke.

"Would you like to tell us about what happened?"

"Do you promise to believe me?" Ben shyly asked.

"Ben, after all the strange things happening with you these last few days, I'll believe anything. Frankly, I'm not sure what's real anymore."

"Mom?"

"Yes, I'll believe you."

"Well," Ben started with confidence, "this morning when Dr. Sanders was leaving I got up and watched through the window as he walked up to Scrawlyknot and . . ."

"Wait. Who's Scrawlyknot?" his father interjected.

"Oh. He's the big creature living underneath the giant oak in the yard."

"The creature under the oak?" his father asked with disbelief in his voice.

"You said you'd promise to believe me!"

"I know, I know. Okay, I just want to understand. I'm listening." His father said, reassuringly.

Ben continued. "Well, I was really surprised to see Scrawlyknot being so playful and knocking Dr. Sanders's hat off his head. I thought he was afraid to let people know he was there, but I guess it's because Dr. Sanders knew him when he was a boy."

His parents turned and stared at each other.

"You don't believe me, do you?"

"In fact, I think we do believe you," said his father. "We saw the oak knock Dr. Sanders's hat off his head, but we . . . it's just we . . . didn't quite know what to make of it. You gotta appreciate that this is um . . . kinda new for us. Know what I mean?"

"Sure. But if you were to meet them you'd know they're the best friends you could ever have. And they're really gentle even though they're big!"

"I'm sure they are. Now tell us, you say Dr. Sanders knows them too?"

Ben hesitated for a moment. He realized he'd accidentally betrayed Dr. Sanders's secret. Was it safe to say more? Listening to his heart, he got his answer. He felt he could trust his parents now.

"Well, when you took me to see Dr. Sanders the other day, and we talked in his office alone, he showed me that he had the same mark on his chest that I have." Ben lifted his pajamas top and pointed to the star shape that glowed and shimmered on his chest. "You see, when he was a little boy the creatures from Nowt came to him too, but then they stopped. He wasn't sure why. When I told him about all the things that had happened to me, he was really excited. But he told me people probably wouldn't understand, and that we should just keep it a secret."

"I see," his mother said. "That explains a few things."

"So anyway, after he left this morning, Scrawlyknot leaned way over to the window and told me all about how things change and die, but not really. Then he touched me with a branch, and I felt this tingling all over, and the scratches and bruises just disappeared. And he talked about growing roots."

Ben's parents were so caught up in the story of how the giant oak had healed Ben with just the touch of a limb that Ben's comment about growing roots was all but lost to them. His father said, "Let me understand something. These creatures who live under the ground, they're the ones you've been playing with late at night and on these adventures in the woods?"

"Not just them. There's Lorno, and Pere, and the stream who talked to me, and the air and all of its secret bubbles, and the Sner-rocks . . ."

"The Sner-rocks?" his father questioned.

"Yeah! They're these huge creatures who look a lot like rocks, but aren't. And down below in the huge cave they blew gigantic bubbles that make everything we know come true. I was able to walk right into one. It was amazing! And Hosoofang the coyote led me out of the woods last night . . ."

"Slow down a second. You say a wild coyote showed you the way home?"

"Um, hm," Ben said, with short, confidant nods of his head.

"I guess that's no harder to believe than creatures living under the ground with trees growing out of their heads," said his father. "But there's something you said earlier that I didn't quite get. About growing roots, and dying and change. What did you mean by that?"

Ben looked down at the blanket, unsure of what to say. Even he didn't understand what it all meant, and the last thing he wanted was to alarm his parents. "Well, I'm not sure. It's just that Scrawlyknot said that sometimes when we change it feels like we're dying, but that's not really what's happening. And I don't really know what he meant about me growing roots. It's just that I had these feelings in my feet. I don't know."

His mother entered the conversation after being silent for the longest time. "You had strange feelings in your feet?"

"Uh, huh."

"Are you still having them?"

"Not right now."

"Let's have a look," she said, pulling back the covers. The bottoms of Ben's feet were covered with red splotches, like measles. When she ran her hand over them, she could feel the slightest little bumps. "Were you walking barefoot in the woods yesterday?"

"No."

"I see. Well, I don't know what's going on with your feet. I really doubt that you're growing roots, though."

"That's what Scrawlyknot said!"

"Yes, I realize that, but little boys don't normally grow roots. They just get into all kinds of things. But then again," she said thoughtfully, "I'm beginning to understand that you're not a normal run-of-the-mill little boy. I'll call Dr. Sanders and see what he has to say. In the meantime, I think you need to eat a little lunch and get some rest. We can talk more about all this later, okay?"

Ben obediently nodded as his mother placed the tray with the soup and sandwich on his lap. His parents slipped out the door without saying a word, but their eyes met and spoke what their hearts had to say. They were confused, amazed, bewildered, and frightened. They came into the kitchen and sat at the table, holding each other's hands. His mother spoke first.

"I'm going to call Dr. Sanders."

"Good idea." His dad twisted his mouth into a tight knot. "He seems to be in on the secret. I'd like to hear his side of the story."

Reaching behind her, she brought the phone to the table and quickly punched in the number. It rang for a long time.

"Hello, doctor's office," came the nasal greeting on the other end of the line.

"Is Dr. Sanders available?"

"He's with a patient. May I ask who is calling and what this is in reference to?"

"This is Ben Jameson's mother. Tell Dr. Sanders something else has come up and I need to talk to him."

"One minute please."

After a long wait, the wise, old voice of Dr. Sanders came on the phone. "Ellen, how's he doing?"

"Well doctor, I think he's fine, except . . . ." Her voice trailed off. She wasn't sure what to say.

"Hello. Hello. Are you still there?" the doctor said.

"Yes Doctor. It's just . . . I don't know quite where to start. I feel foolish saying this but Ben seems to think . . . ."

"Yes?"

"Well, he seems to think that he may be growing . . . roots from the bottom of his feet. I know this is ridiculous, but we kinda believe him. Actually, we don't know what to believe anymore." Her words began to rush out amid tears and sobbing. "With all this talk about creatures under the earth, and spheres of air, and birds and coyotes, and the large tree knocking the hat off your head and . . ."

"Oh, you saw the tree knock the hat off my head this morning?"

"Why, yes, John and I both did. Is it true that there are creatures under the trees? Or is my son, is my son . . . ." Now her tears began to rain down even harder and she handed the phone to her husband.

"Doctor, this is John."

"Is she all right?"

John looked over at his wife. She forced a smile through the tears. "She's okay. This whole thing has been quite a strain for both of us."

"Yes, understandably."

"We're really worried."

"Listen, I think we need to talk. How about if I come around at dinner time and take a look at Ben, and I'll try to tell you what I know about all this. Let me say though that Ben's going to be fine. He's just . . . well, exceptional. In some ways Ben's a normal little boy, but he's been chosen to play a special role in this life. Let me assure you again, he's going to be fine. Be sure he gets plenty of rest today, because, well, it'll be easier to explain later. If anything else comes up and you need me, don't hesitate to call."

Ben's dad heard the click at the other end of the line, but he didn't hang up at first. He stared into the receiver as though something very important were still going to come out of it. Ben's mom lowered her chin, curiously waiting for the verdict.

"Well?"

"He said he'd come by later tonight to have a talk with us and take a look at Ben. He kept on saying that Ben was going to be fine, but . . . ."

"But what?"

"It's just that he said Ben is special, and that he has some work to do in the world."

"What kind of work?"

"I don't really know what he meant. He just said he'd talk about it later, but that there was nothing to worry about."

Reaching out across the table to hold her hands, Ben's father closed his eyes. For the first time in years, he silently prayed for Ben's protection. The wilting rose that had been sitting on the window these last few days suddenly perked up and filled with new life and color. Unfortunately, both of them were so worried about Ben that they missed this miracle, a sign that their prayers had been answered.

Chapter 14

Ben spent that day quietly in bed. When he wasn't sleeping he was engaged in serious discussions with Thurston.

"When we were down in the cave, where did you run after you jumped from my arms, you silly coward?"

"Me, afraid? Not in the least!"

"Well, you certainly made tracks fast," Ben said, squinting at him with one eye.

"I must admit I did feel some concern, but quite truthfully I kept an eye on you for the longest time. Until one of those drat bubbles caught up with me. Once inside I couldn't help myself. It was a cat's dream! So many things to chase, but I never could quite get them to stay in my mouth. Then out of nowhere, this huge, ferocious, cat-eating mouse came right for my throat. Such a battle! If I hadn't fallen out of the bubble I'm certain I would have won."

"So that's what you were up to. Fighting mice after you promised me you wouldn't!"

"I only said I'd keep my paws off that filthy little Lorno. I didn't say a word about other mice. Besides, I was defending myself. It was either me or him!"

"All right. But you realize you were fighting a dream and not a real mouse."

"It was too real to be a dream!"

"I know, but everything in the bubbles are dreams out of which the world is made. And because you insisted on fighting, cats and mice will probably be at each other's throats for another thousand years."

"Oh my! I never realized that I was responsible for every cat and mouse fight in the world. Oh goodness gracious me. Is there nothing I can do?"

Ben paused for a moment. "There is one thing, but I don't think you're ready to meet the challenge."

"Who, me? There's not a thing I cannot do or be! Now tell me of this challenge and I'll even sacrifice one of my lives if I have to."

"While in the bubbles I learned that if a cat like you could travel around the world three times, and bring back to me the petal of a flower from every land, then peace between earth and man can stretch for generations like the desert sand."

"You expect me to travel throughout the world with no food or place to sleep in search of flower petals? Why, who would feed me? And how do you know for sure these things will happen? Moreover, the thought that cats would no longer eat mice is one of the most disgusting, outrageous, idiotic things I've ever heard."

"Ah, just as I suspected. You're not up for the task. I'll have to find someone else. Perhaps . . . Lorno would be interested."

"That foolish mouse! Why, he wouldn't know where to turn once he left those woods. He'd be gobbled up by the first cat who spied his juicy tail."

"Maybe so. I suppose I will have to find someone to protect him on his journey. It would have to be someone crafty, someone wise to the ways of the world. Someone quick on his feet, but with the patience to travel on the currents of time. Do you know such a person?"

"Well . . ." Thurston cleared his throat. ". . . the only one I know who is qualified for such a journey is . . . well, I am not boasting now, but truthfully, I am the one for the job. I know of no person or cat who even comes close to fitting that description. Not to say that I would take the job now, mind you. I'm just stating a fact."

"Oh no," said Ben. "I would never ask you to undertake such a dangerous assignment. Besides, I understand that in some parts of the world they don't even have canned cat food. They force cats to live off fresh fish, liver, and turkey. Such a terrible fate."

"Fresh fish, liver, and turkey? Did you say fresh fish, liver, and turkey?" Thurston licked his lips.

Ben nodded emphatically. "It's terrible, don't you think?"

"Oh, I agree, most wholeheartedly! It's a shame that I don't know a cat for miles who likes to eat such things. On occasion I can force myself, you know. Not that such foods agree with my sensitive stomach, but I am capable of making sacrifices." Thurston glanced off into the distance as he spoke. He quickly looked out of the corner of his eye to see if he had hoodwinked Ben.

"Do you mean that after all, you might consider making this trip with Lorno?"

"Well, given that I am the most qualified, and with such awful food I know you'll never be able to enlist anyone else to travel under such conditions. Now, you are certain that all they have in these lands is fresh fish, liver, and turkey?"

"Oh yes, quite certain!"

"Well, in that case, in the name of our friendship I will make the sacrifice to undertake this journey. When do we leave?"

"With the rising sun tomorrow morning."

"I see. In that case I better gather together my belongings and make preparations. I have a few goodbyes to say as well. If you don't mind, I'll speak to you later."

"Oh, certainly. I understand. Thank you for reconsidering."

Thurston jumped from the bed and scampered down the stairs. Ben could hear the cat door swing open and shut. He chuckled to himself, then thought, now there's just Lorno to convince. Even though he knew it would be more difficult to get him to agree to this incredible journey, he had a plan he was certain would work. But it would have to wait for later. Shutting his eyes, he slowly drifted back to sleep.

When Ben woke, he could feel his mother's cool hand on his forehead. Through dreamy eyes he looked into her face. "My," she said, "I've never seen you sleep so long. How are you feeling?"

Ben moaned and stretched. "Okay, I guess. What time is it?"

"Nearly seven o'clock. Are you hungry?"

Ben thought for a minute. He was and he wasn't. Strangely, the hungry feelings were in the bottom of his feet as well as his stomach. He bobbed his head up and down as he shrugged his shoulders.

"Let me use my magical powers to discern this sign. You're kind of hungry but not really sure what you want to eat?"

"Yeah," Ben replied. "How'd you guess?"

"Oh, it takes many years of training at mother school."

Ben smiled.

"How about some turkey casserole and steamed carrots? Maybe a little salad, too?"

Ben scrunched up his face, but nodded. Carrots were his least favorite vegetable.

"Do you want to come downstairs or eat in bed?"

"I'll come downstairs."

"Good. And why don't you put on some clothes. I think it'll make you feel better." She gave him a pat on the head and turned to leave.

"Say, Mom?"

"Yes, honey?"

"Do you think it's possible for people to grow in the ground like trees?"

His mom paused and looked at the floor as she contemplated this unusual question. "Well, if you'd asked me yesterday, I probably would have said no. But today . . . I'm not so sure. If they did live in the ground I don't know how they'd eat, or whether they'd have branches coming out of their ears or if they ever could run around again like other little boys." She bit her lower lip. "What makes you ask?"

"Oh, I don't know. Just something I've been thinking about."

"I tell you what. Dr. Sanders is coming over soon. He seems to be wise in these things. Why don't you ask him?"

"Yeah, I bet he would know!"

"I bet he would, too. When you're ready, get dressed and come on downstairs."

When Ben's mom walked into the kitchen where his dad was seated at the table, tears were welling up in her eyes. She sat facing him.

"Something wrong?"

"Oh, I don't know. I have this terrible feeling. Something's getting ready to happen and I don't think I'm going to like it."

"What went on up there?"

"Nothing really. It's just that he wanted to know if little boys could grow roots and live in the ground like trees."

"Well, that's certainly imaginative," his dad replied, chuckling to himself.

"John, I don't think it's funny."

"I know there's been a lot of strange things happening these last few days, but you don't seriously think that such a thing's possible? What's gotten into you?"

"I don't know. It's just . . . this odd feeling I have that we're going to lose Ben. I already feel like we've lost him. I've been thinking back over the last few days, and how much he's been talking about his friends from Nowt. Did I tell you that the other day there were muddy footprints leading from his window to his bed, but nowhere else in his room? Explain to me, John, how a seven-year old boy could get mud on his feet, walk inside, up the stairs to the window, and only then start tracking mud. The only way that it could have happened is if someone, or something, lifted him up to the window. Explain that to me."

Ben's dad sat silently, looking at the table top. He looked out the window. There, sitting on the sill, was the rose that Ben had brought in days before, as fresh as though it had just been picked. It had sprouted two additional buds which were now beginning to bloom. He got up and walked to the window to take a closer look. Lifting the vase he turned to her. "I don't recall there being any other buds on this rose the other day. Did you replace this with a fresh rose?"

She shook her head. He stood there for nearly a minute, examining the flowers from every angle. Shaking his head in bewilderment, he returned the vase to the window sill. Leaning against the counter while crossing his arms, he said, "I don't know anymore. Perhaps we're the ones who are going crazy."

"John, I know you think that this is strange, but . . . would you come with me and . . . talk with the oak tree outside?"

He cocked his head and bit the side of his lip. "Do what?"

"Yeah," she said, nodding her head and lifting her shoulders, looking for his approval.

"Sure, why not. I would hate to think that everyone in my family is good friends with the trees except me." Reluctantly, he followed her out the door, across the yard, to the base of the huge oak. They both stood there silently looking up into the tree's limbs. She looked over to him self-consciously.

"Do you suppose it can hear us?"

"I don't have any proof that it can't. My, what big ears you have, Grandma."

"This isn't a joke. Please be serious."

"Okay, it's just that I feel ridiculous standing here talking to a tree."

"How do you think I feel? But maybe there's something this tree can teach us."

"All right, but you do the talking."

She turned back to face the tree and took a deep breath, then let it out. "I don't know if you can hear us, but we're Ben's mom and dad. We're worried about Ben. He's . . . he's told us about you and your kingdom, and, well, frankly we didn't believe him at first. But so many strange things have been happening over the past few days that, we don't quite know what to think anymore. We thought . . . we thought . . ." She stumbled on her words and began to cry again. Ben's dad put his arm around her.

Clearing his throat, he said, "It's . . . it's just that we thought you could help us. We feel like we're losing our little boy, and we're scared. We don't know where to turn, and if you're real, truly real, we need you to help us. Please."

As they stood there the tree hung its limbs in silence. Ben's mom cried even harder. "Why don't you speak to us?" she pleaded.

The old oak trembled, slowly at first, hardly noticeable to them. Then the tremble turned into a shaking, and the limbs swayed back and forth even though there wasn't any wind in the air. They looked up at the tree, their sorrow turning quickly to fear.

"What's happening?" Ellen whispered.

John didn't say a word. Tears now filled his eyes.

She tugged at him. Taking a short step away, Ben's parents found their path blocked by a large limb bending down from the top of the tree. They quickly turned to face it. The limb nudged them toward the tree's trunk, gently, but with authority. Within three steps they were pinned against Scrawlyknot.

"John, do something!"

Another branch reached down, quivering before their faces. They both closed their eyes, grimacing, expecting something terrible to happen. But what they felt was entirely a surprise.

Slowly, gently, the branch caressed their cheeks, wiping away the tears. Neither could remember ever being touched with such loving care, even by their mothers. Their feelings of fear and sadness melted away as they relaxed into the tree's warm embrace.

Blending his voice right in with their cozy feelings, Scrawlyknot sang them a wispy, treemungerman song. "Sah, sah woh woo hoo. Hyee, roh loh toh coo. Keedee, shah nah, hah yah sah ho coo. Keedee, yee rah lah noo." Again and again he repeated this song. "Sah, sah woh woo hoo. Hyee, roh loh toh coo. Keedee, shah nah, hah yah sah ho coo. Keedee, yee rah lah noo." A sweet smile appeared on their faces.

Ben's dad reached up and gently ran his hand across the branch that lightly held him. He didn't know why, but he suddenly loved this tree as though it were part of his family. With his other hand he reached out and gently caressed his wife's arm. She thought it was the tree.

Scrawlyknot whispered his song more and more softly, until there was only silence. Pulling his limbs away, he released them from his hold. Opening their eyes at the same time, they stared blankly into the space in front of them. Out of the corner of his eye, Ben's dad looked at his wife. Out of the corner of her eye, she looked at him. They both giggled like two children.

Scrawlyknot interrupted their peaceful gaze with his soft, purring voice. "Now, you know our secret. The treemungermen have returned to this land to bring new life to you. Now that you know what it is to be free of doubt, you can let your son take root with his friends from Nowt. There are no worries to overcome. What you lose can only grow into a treasure for all the world under the sun. What appears to change on the outward surface, fulfills all that is for a higher purpose." He paused for a moment. "Dr. Sanders is on his way. Greet him. Share with him all that has happened. He will understand and prepare you, guarding Ben's life even in the time of decay."

The tree straightened its branches. The sun drooped below the horizon casting a pale, orange light over everything. Ben's parents looked at each other and embraced in a way they had never done before. They held each other as though it were the last time. Neither wanted to move.

Chapter 15

When the headlights of Dr. Sanders's car swung into the drive, Ben's parents turned and were blinded by the bright glare. As the car pulled to a stop they could see who it was. After Dr. Sanders stepped from the car, he stared at them with a strange expression, quizzing them with his eyes.

"You both all right?" he asked, walking slowly toward them.

They didn't reply.

"Something wrong?"

Together, they half shook their heads. Dr. Sanders stopped two paces away. "Something's happened that you need to tell me about, hasn't it?"

They nodded, but still didn't utter a word.

"Now folks, is there a reason you're not talking or are we going to stand out here all night while I guess?"

Finally, Ben's dad found his tongue. "You're not going to believe what's just happened to us."

"Try me," Dr. Sanders said with quiet reassurance.

His father searched for the right words. He suddenly realized how foolish he felt explaining the events of the last few minutes to another adult. Would Dr. Sanders think they had lost their mind? Would he believe them?

"Well?" Dr. Sanders interjected as he waited for an answer.

"You see, we came out here to have a talk with the. . . the tree. Ellen felt that, well, we had seen you talking to the tree earlier and we thought maybe, um, maybe . . ." His voice trailed off.

Ben's Mom broke in with newfound confidence. "We thought the tree could help us. I know it sounds foolish, but Doctor, we were really desperate. It just seemed like the right thing to do."

"And what happened?" Dr. Sanders asked, looking over the rim of his glasses.

"At first the tree shook and trembled, and then we moved away from it. Suddenly the path was blocked by large branches leaning down to the ground. We were frightened. They started pushing us back toward the tree until we were pinned against the trunk. Then it started." As she said these last words her attention seemed to drift off to another place, another time. She stared ahead vacantly.

"What started?"

She snapped out of her daydream. "The singing. The tree sang us a lullaby. It wasn't like anything I'd ever heard before. I can still hear it. I've never felt so peaceful, so alive. The love in my heart kept growing bigger and bigger. I can't describe how wonderful it was." Once again, that expression came over her face as her eyes softly glazed over.

"Did the tree say anything to you?"

She nodded, then shook her head.

"It did and it didn't?"

"Yes, it did. But I didn't understand what it meant." She paused. "It spoke of strange things. Of Ben taking root, and his life being devoted to a higher purpose. He even talked about you guarding Ben's life during a time of decay. Do you know what that means?"

Ben's dad angrily burst out, "What do you know that you haven't been telling us? You're friends with these, these trees, or creatures. Why are they here? Why have they chosen Ben? Why do they have to turn our life upside-down?" He was furious, getting redder and redder in the face with each passing moment.

Dr. Sanders placed his hand upon Ben's father's chest and looked deeply into his eyes. "John, calm yourself. There will be plenty of time to answer all your questions." Ben's dad looked squarely into the doctor's face, and relaxed.

"I'm sorry. I suddenly felt panicked. I don't know what happened."

"It's all right. If I had been through what you both have been through the last few minutes, I think I would have been a little scared, too. Let's get inside and sit down. Then we can talk more and sort this out. There's a lot I have to say to you, and there are some things that only Ben can answer." With his arms wrapped around each of their shoulders, he led them slowly across the yard to the back door.

As though they were children, he sat them down at the kitchen table, put the kettle on to boil, then went to the stairs and called to Ben. "Ben, you up there?" At first there was no answer. "Ben?"

"Yes, Dr. Sanders," came a meek reply.

"Can you join me and your parents down in the kitchen?"

"I . . . I don't know."

"What do you mean you don't know?"

"It's just that my feet have these little bumps on them."

Hm, thought Dr. Sanders. It's begun sooner than I expected. "Wait right there and let me come up and take a look." He bounded up the stairs like a child. Ben was sitting on the edge of the bed, now dressed, with tears rolling down his cheeks. The doctor sat next to him and pulled him close. Ben nearly melted into his arms. After a few minutes of holding him, Dr. Sanders said, "Let me a take a look at those feet."

Ben slid back on the bed and held up one foot. Just as he had said, there were little red bumps covering his sole. Dr. Sanders ran his hand along his heel, then up to his toes, slowly massaging the skin. "Well Ben, you know what these are, don't you?"

Ben nodded. "Roots?"

"Yep. Roots."

"Will I ever be able to run and play again."

"I don't rightly know. But I do know that you're going to be able to do things and feel feelings and think thoughts that no one else in the world can. You're special. What the treemungermen have in store for you is more incredible than anything either of us could ever imagine. You see, you're the first person in thousands of years to return to the Kingdom of Nowt. I envy you."

Ben wiped his nose with the back of his hand. "What are my mom and dad going to say?"

"Oh, I think our friend Scrawlyknot has taken care of that. Your parents got to meet him a few minutes ago, or should I say, were touched by him. They're downstairs still recovering. I think you'll find they'll believe your stories now. There's much to talk about, and time is short. Let's join them. What do you say?"

Ben nodded in agreement.

"Can you walk?"

"I think so. It just feels funny."

"Hm. What an adventure you're about to take young man. I'd trade places with you at the drop of a hat. If only I were sixty years younger. Well," he said, heaving a big sigh, "your parents must be wondering where in the world we are. Up we go." He helped Ben to his feet.

"It's not so bad," Ben said, as he walked to the door and back, like a person taking his first steps after having a cast removed. Together they reached the top of the stairs. Dr. Sanders put his hand on Ben's shoulder and held him back for a minute. "Your parents have been through a nasty shock. Don't say anything about the bottom of your feet yet. I don't want to alarm them." Ben gave him a short nod as they made their way down the stairs, one by one.

When Ben came into the kitchen his mother spread her arms wide and he ran to her. She held him tightly, gently rocking him back and forth, kissing his neck and cooing in his ear. It had been a long time since she had done that. Ben's dad watched with tears in his eyes. Dr. Sanders stood in the doorway with a thin smile on his face. His eyes weren't dry either.

Blowing his nose with his big handkerchief, Dr. Sanders broke the silence. "Now folks, there's an awful lot to talk about tonight, and quite frankly, I'm getting hungry. Seeing all that food on the stove makes me think we ought to do some eating before we start talking."

Ben's mom looked up, then gave Ben one more squeeze. He slid from her lap and crawled into his father's waiting arms. She got up and set the table, wiping her eyes with her apron every minute or so. Dinner was served in no time and they ate under a strained silence.

Ben's appetite was ravenous. He couldn't seem to get enough. His dad made a joking comment. "Son, you're eating like it's your last meal." Both Dr. Sanders and Ben's mom looked up from their plates. His father stopped chewing and quickly swallowed what was in his mouth. Scratching the back of his head, he smiled nervously, then went back to eating.

After the plates were cleared, Ben's mom suggested they go into the living room where it was more comfortable. When Dr. Sanders sat on the loveseat facing the couch, Ben crawled up beside him. His mom and dad sat down opposite them, hands folded in their laps, apprehensive about what was to follow.

Dr. Sanders cleared his throat. "I'm not sure where to begin. Perhaps it's best I tell you what I know, then let Ben tell us in his own words all that has happened, and what is to be." Ben's parents just looked as though they were gazing right through him. "Okay?" he asked.

They both nodded with trance-like expressions.

"Well, when I was a boy, not much younger than Ben, I grew up just down the road from here when all this was farmland," he said, with the sweep of his hand. My parents and I moved when I was seven. When I heard what happened to Ben, it all became real clear. You see, when I was his age, it also happened to me." Dr. Sanders smiled at Ben. With that large arm of his, the doctor pulled Ben closer, and continued.

"By some strange twist of fate, Ben and I are like brothers. When I was his age, the treemungermen also came to me one night. For months I would sneak out my window, and play and dance with Scrawlyknot and all his friends from Nowt until the early morning hours. My parents, like you, started to worry. They were alarmed by my tales of adventure with these strange creatures. They were simple folks. Such stories confused them. One night, though, my father woke and stepped outdoors to find me dangling from the uppermost limbs of Scrawlyknot's head. His screams brought the dancing and singing to a screeching halt. All the creatures of Nowt turned to face him. Scrawlyknot gently lowered me to the ground. My dad, a brave soul, marched right up to Scrawlyknot and said in a resounding voice, 'If you don't mind, I'd like to have a word with you in private.' I stood like a frozen statue. Scrawlyknot nodded and marched off behind my father into the cornfields. They must have talked for an hour while each of the creatures stood quietly, not moving or shaking a limb. When they returned, my father put his arm around my shoulder, and said, 'Say good-bye now to your friends, because they're not going to be coming around anymore.' Crying, I begged my dad to not let this happen. Then, I turned to Scrawlyknot, and he just nodded and said, 'It's best Timothy. But one day you will return and dance with us like you never danced before. Don't forget, you are the door, the way, a healer of the one to follow another day.' Slowly they all returned to the earth as my father and I watched them disappear. He had to hold me back as Scrawlyknot was the last to crawl into his hole in the ground, leaving nothing in view but the trunk which grew out of his crown. It's hard to believe that a child could cry as much as

I did in the days that followed, but just seeing a tree or bush would bring tears to my eyes.

My parents decided that it would be best that we move to get me away from all those memories. When we left, it did help in a way. I made new friends, and after a while, I began wondering if the Kingdom of Nowt really existed. All I had was this reminder." Dr. Sanders unbuttoned his shirt and pulled it back, revealing the strange mark on his chest that was exactly like the one Ben had.

Ben's parents leaned forward, their eyes riveted on the distinct design that seemed to glow at the edges. Ben lifted his shirt to his chin revealing his as well. They were identical.

Dr. Sanders re-buttoned his shirt. Ben followed his lead and pulled his shirt down. His parents, though, still sat, gawking.

"Now, I know you'd like a nice tidy explanation of this whole thing. Something full of common sense that could explain it away. In the last few days I've given great thought to this whole matter. The fact is that the Kingdom of Nowt does exist, and probably existed well before we humans ever stepped on this earth. I believe they know more about us and dinosaurs and the history of the world than any scientist could ever know. And they are guided by something even loftier than you and I can imagine. If we could only stop chopping off the tops of their heads and polluting their earth, they could teach us how to live and truly be at home with ourselves. That's . . . where your son comes in."

Dr. Sanders paused for a minute, looking intently into their eyes. Ben turned his gaze from Dr. Sanders to his parents, and then down to his feet, which were beginning to itch and throb.

"This is an extraordinary time," Dr. Sanders continued. "For some reason that you and I probably will never understand, Ben has been chosen to play a special role in the healing of this world of ours. I can't tell you why or how. It's part of the mystery, I guess. Now, as parents, giving your only son to something like this . . . is hard. But I can promise you that generations to come will thank you."

Ben's dad raised his hand. "What exactly are we giving Ben to?" he asked, apprehensively.

Dr. Sanders looked deeply into Ben's eyes, and Ben nodded.

It was Ben who spoke up now, with a ring of authority in his voice that sent chills down his parents' spines. Even Dr. Sanders was surprised at the maturity of someone so young. "Mother, Dad, I know that I have disobeyed you often in the last few days, and I've seen the worry on your faces. I was torn because I had to obey someone else. As Scrawlyknot has said, it is He whom we serve. Sometimes we're asked to be more than who we are. To fly higher in the sky than we can even imagine. To reach into the earth where life remakes itself, even when we try to destroy it. Since first meeting the treemungermen, I've changed. Every day their songs have crept into my heart, and I feel like I've grown bigger than I am. I love these creatures and the earth where they live. I want to be close to them. To protect them. To teach people to understand what a magical place this really is. You must understand me and accept the things that are about to happen. Remember, I will always be nearby waiting for your touch and your loving words."

"Everyone keeps talking about something that's going to happen. Would someone please explain to me what you mean?" His mother's voice quivered.

Ben and Dr. Sanders looked into each other's eyes for what seemed to be the longest time. Ben turned to his mother. "You know how you taught me that butterflies start out as caterpillars and slowly weave a cocoon before they become a beautiful thing? Something like that is about to happen to me. I am going to rejoin the treemungermen and return to the age when the People of Luan deeply rooted themselves in the earth."

His mother interrupted him. "You're going to grow roots like a tree?"

Ben nodded.

She turned and faced the doctor. "Dr. Sanders? Human beings don't grow roots! It's impossible!"

"I realize that . . . it's rather peculiar, but I can assure you that this is happening as we speak. Actually, it's one of the most amazing things that ever happened on the face of the earth. Don't you see that Ben has been chosen to teach all of us in a way that we have never been able to learn before? People will come from every corner of the earth to sit under his branches."

Both his mother and father spoke up at the same time. "His branches!"

"I'm afraid so. Since he soon won't be eating or breathing like you and me, he'll have to get his nourishment from the sun and the air. He'll need branches, all right."

Ben's parents sank back in the couch, dumbfounded. Dr. Sanders shrugged his shoulders and raised his eyebrows in Ben's direction. Ben, too, shrugged his shoulders. Dr. Sanders cleared his throat twice before turning back to them. "I see that this has been quite a shock. Now, John and Ellen, what you're thinking and feeling is perfectly normal. Having a son growing out of the ground is not exactly the dream of every parent. But think of it. All the world coming to learn from Ben! Doesn't that make you proud?"

Their faces were pale. Ben thought they might be getting sick.

Dr. Sanders hurriedly continued, seemingly ignoring their dreadful reaction. "Of course, you need to be prepared for all that is to happen in the next few days. I must say, though, that we need to put Ben's welfare above all else."

If they heard him, none of what he said seemed to make an impression. He didn't have time, though, to wait for their reply. The appointed hour was approaching.

Ben motioned to Dr. Sanders with his finger. The doctor leaned over as Ben whispered into his ear. He nodded in agreement. Ben got up and sat down on the coffee table facing his parents. He peacefully looked into their eyes. "If you listen to the quiet beat of your heart, it will guide you every step of the way. At times you may want to run, at times you may want to cling. But in the end I promise you together we will sing. As I grow, tall and true, and change my face, nothing I become will lessen my love for you. When you see my friends from Nowt, you'll understand, that what I do is for every man, woman, and child, for generations to come. I am here to save this land. Trust me. Trust your hearts. For me there will be no pain, even when my legs grow lame. In their place will grow a trunk strong and old. And through my mouth the wisdom of the earth will speak, erasing all doubt that Luan and Nowt are brought back together again. I am the symbol. I am the one. It is my lot to become a treemungerman. I can no longer be your son."

Ben got up, wedged himself between his parents, and for a few moments they cuddled him like the small child they had always known. Together they sat as a family for the last time.

Chapter 16

From the door came a tapping. Both of Ben's parents looked at Dr. Sanders with apprehension, then stared frightfully at each other. "Should we answer it?" asked his father.

Dr. Sanders nodded. Another knock came from the door. Ben's dad stood and walked into the foyer. As he opened the door a large gust of wind blasted in, blowing leaves and dust into the living room. He stood there, silhouetted by the door frame, searching the night for something like a tree, but bigger. He could see nothing. Turning and laughing nervously, he said, "There's nobody here."

"Are you sure?" asked Dr. Sanders.

"It must've been the wind." At that moment something brushed against his shoulder. He turned back to face the door, but still could see nothing. "I think I'm losing my mind," he whispered to himself, as he walked out on the porch.

Then he saw it, bigger than anything he could have imagined. It was breathtaking. He looked up its legs to its mammoth torso and finally to the magnificent face smiling down at him.

Ben's mom called out to him, "John, are you all right?"

Walking to the door, she stopped on the threshold. "John? Is there something wrong?" He still didn't respond. She walked to his side and said, "Jo . . . ." His name trailed off into the wind as she too saw the giant creature towering above her. Looking up, she stared at their mysterious visitor, unable to move.

Meanwhile, Dr. Sanders and Ben had come to the door. The moon's light tore through the clouds and lit up Scrawlyknot from behind, accentuating his height as he stood nearly four times the size of the house. Ben's mother gasped. Under his breath, Dr. Sanders said, "He's bigger than I remembered."

Scrawlyknot spoke. His booming voice rattled the windows. "It's a mighty fine evening, isn't it?" Both of Ben's parents stepped back fearfully. Then he laughed. "It is a mighty fine evening. A good night for planting the seeds of friendship, don't you think!" He chuckled as he turned to Ben. "I believe introductions are in order, are they not my fellow treemungerman?"

Ben stepped forward proudly next to his parents. He reached out and took his mother's hand. Instinctively, she took his dad's hand. "Scrawlyknot, I'd like to introduce you to my mom and dad. Mom and Dad, this is my best friend in the whole world, Scrawlyknot."

His parents half bowed to the giant creature. Scrawlyknot graciously returned the bow. Then Ben motioned to Dr. Sanders who stepped forward. "I think you two already know each other." Dr. Sanders smile was beaming.

"Ah, yes, Timothy Sanders, I remember you well. It was a sad day for me when you left this dell, but it gladdens my heart to see you again, especially on a night like this when our worlds twine together, loosening the grip of yesterday's fetters. My little Timothy, you don't mind if I call you Timothy, do you?"

"No, not at all," chirped Dr. Sanders. His face had taken on a boyish glow, and he stood tall and straight, like the seven-year old that Scrawlyknot remembered.

"Ah, good. You know, you haven't changed a bit. Do you remember the time we played pick-up sticks?"

"Remember it? I've never had so much fun in my whole life!" said Dr. Sanders.

"Me too," said Scrawlyknot. "It had been five thousand years since I laughed so hard." He chuckled heartily, and the gleam of the moon reflected off his shiny, white teeth. A passing cloud blocked out the light, and Scrawlyknot's laughter turned into a stern frown. Pointing to Dr. Sanders, he said seriously, "Timothy, I doubt that you would have ever guessed the role you are to play today. You are the protector. It is you who must keep the wolves at bay, caring for our little sapling so that his roots may grow deep. This is my charge. Until twelve new moons pass through the sky, I command you to never let this child of Nowt far from your watchful eye."

Dr. Sanders obediently nodded.

"Thank you, Timothy." Scrawlyknot reached out and touched Dr. Sanders's head. A bright light flowed through Scrawlyknot's hand and encircled Dr. Sanders for a just a second, and then it was gone!

Scrawlyknot next turned to Ben's parents. They rocked self-consciously from foot to foot. Sheepishly, they cast their eyes to the ground. "So, what shall we do with you?"

Looking up, they both shrugged.

"Ah, words are often hard to find in the night, especially if you are parents of a treemungerman. It's quite a responsibility. And you thought you were just ordinary people," he said, chuckling once again.

"We thought we were," Ben's father feebly replied.

"Hmm," pondered Scrawlyknot. "It's often what we are blind to that brings us the greatest gifts." Scrawlyknot paused. "You search my face for answers where there are none. There's much to learn, my dear friends, but you have to believe in order to take the first step. Open your hearts and let your eyes see far into the distance. The sacrifice that I ask of you tonight will be repaid when it averts the blight."

"I don't understand," piped up Ben's dad.

"Stop thinking like a man. Instead, think like the land. What would the land do if it could speak and act like you!"

"Well . . . it probably would have a lot to say to me about what I do for a living?"

"Exactly! And the reason the land is begging for your son is that it needs a voice to be heard by all people, that they may understand and think with land-spirit, feel with land-heart, and see with land-eyes."

Ben's dad nodded in recognition.

"He's my son! You can't take him!" cried Ben's mother.

Scrawlyknot reached out and lightly caressed her cheek. Kindness was etched on his face. "Yes. It is a greater sacrifice for you. Living so long in the bosom of our mother earth, I know your pain. That's why you must not stop being a mother. Your son will continue to need your love, and for a while, even food to sustain him. I ask of you, embrace this change for my people, and yours."

Looking up into his loving face, she wiped away her tears as Scrawlyknot rained leaves down from the tree resting on his head. He held her hand for quite some time before turning to Ben.

"Ah, my little friend. So brave to stand with us and do battle, to carry our mantle. We have waited thousands of years for this moment, patiently biding our time beneath the earth's crust, sleeping like those who have returned to dust. But now we rejoice, for the world is about to embark on a journey out of the dark. Come, climb upon my shoulders. Stand on my branches and greet your newfound friends."

Ben grabbed Scrawlyknot's fingers and climbed into his palm. Carefully, the huge creature lifted him to the tallest branches in the tree sprouting from his head. Ben grabbed hold of a limb and held on tightly. He could see deep into the night sky. The clouds rushing by were nearly within reach.

In the distance, two black specks approached. He guessed who they were—Pere, the falcon, and Eagle. They landed, one on each side of Ben. Reaching out both of his hands, he petted their heads and their backs.

"Pere, Eagle," Ben said, "I'm going to become a treemungerman, and won't be able to fly anymore . . . but, you're always welcome to land in my branches."

Eagle spoke. "Ben, sorely we will yearn for those days as well. But the appointed hour has not yet arrived, there is still time to fly! Join us one last time, that we may remember your company. Fill the air with your magical song, so that the others below may know what it means to fly against all that is wrong."

Ben closed his eyes, and thought the magical flying words. He lifted off the branch a few inches, hovering in mid-air. Out loud he sang, "Sah yah harh woo hooo, Ben lah ho lah doo. Ahziz ruhr, caliz duhr. Antai yo, antai yo. Yee cohr rie, lisso mee. Yom!" With arms outstretched, he flew from the tree like a large bird. Eagle and Pere followed close behind.

Below them Dr. Sanders yelled to Ben's parents with his finger stretched skyward. They both gasped as they saw their son disappearing into the thick clouds overhead.

His mother yelled, "What was that?"

"That, my dear lady, was your son!" said Dr. Sanders.

"My son? Flying?"

"Indeed. Now that's something I'd give my eye teeth to do."

Ben, Eagle and Pere came swooping out of the darkness at over a hundred miles per hour. They screeched across the open yard just a few feet above his parents and Dr. Sanders, then disappeared into the night.

"John. Our son can fly. Imagine. He can fly!" she screamed, with newfound pride.

Ben's dad was dumbfounded.

Everyone, including Scrawlyknot, scoured the sky for a glimpse of Ben and his escorts. All they could see was the moon occasionally breaking through the cloud's cover.

"Where is he?" his mom asked. "Do you see him?"

Dr. Sanders said, "He'll be back."

"Is it safe? I mean, he won't fall or anything, will he?"

"Safe? Of course it is," said Scrawlyknot. "Why don't you try it for yourself."

"What? Me fly? Oh, no, no, no," she said, waving her hands in front of her.

"I insist. If you are going to be the mother of the most remarkable child on this earth, you must know that magic lurks at every turn. To fly will fulfill everything for which you yearn. To be a lark will make you what we treemungermen know as lolly-folly-tolly smart. Come now. It's easy. I'll ask Eagle to teach you."

Scrawlyknot lifted his head to the sky and bellowed, "Yom mobarry, ho ho my!" Two panes of glass broke in the house from the strength of his voice. Ben's parents and Dr. Sanders cowered back a few steps.

From above, somewhere in the clouds, an eagle screeched. Suddenly, the clouds parted and the moon's light broke through. There, silhouetted against the lunar face, were three figures. They hovered for a moment, then turned and headed right toward where everyone was standing. With barely a sound, Ben, Pere, and Eagle landed softly on the ground.

Pere and Eagle raised their wings to Scrawlyknot, then to Ben's parents and Dr. Sanders. Both of his parents awkwardly raised their arms. Dr. Sanders, though, bowed deeply and gracefully.

"Mom, Dad, Dr. Sanders, I'd like to introduce you to Eagle and Pere. They're the ones who stood by me the day I stayed up in the tree. And it was Eagle who taught me to fly. I've never had two better friends."

"Thank you for your kind words," said Eagle. "It is we, though, who are grateful to have served you so."

"You can talk?" Ben's dad stammered.

"Why, yes," Pere squawked. "We have always talked to you. But now, you can hear, whereas before you were deafened by fear."

"And, and you can understand us?"

"Of course."

"And Ben, they taught you to fly?" his mother interjected.

"Yeah, Mom. It's easy. Eagle could teach you to fly, too."

"Yes," said Scrawlyknot, "I think it would be good for our new friends to experience the sky."

"Oh mighty treemungerman, I agree," said Eagle. "As soon as they see this earth from above, they're sure to fill it with love. Come, stand by me, and speak the secret words that will lift your feet from the ground, allowing you to enter the heavens in search of all that is unfound. Sah yah harh woo hooo, Ellen, John, Timothy, lah ho lah doo. Ahziz ruhr, caliz duhr. Antai yo, antai yo. Yee cohr rie, lisso mee. Yom!"

"What?" they all asked with anticipation.

"Listen closely and repeat after me. Sah yah hahr woo hooo."

"Sah yah hahr woo hooo," they said in unison.

"Now, say your name, then 'lah ho lah doo'."

Each said his name and repeated after Eagle, "Lah ho lah doo."

Ben's mom was the first to giggle. "My feet, they're tingling. I feel, I feel . . . ." Before she could say another word, she rose from the ground, hovering like a hummingbird. Dr. Sanders lifted up as well, followed immediately by Ben's dad. They were laughing like children.

Eagle flapped his powerful wings. They halted their laughter. "That's better now. Flying is indeed fun, but remember never to fly too close to the sun."

They shook their heads and their bodies waved back and forth. A giggle slipped from Ben's mom. "I'm sorry. I'm sorry," she said, trying to hold back her excitement.

Eagle cleared his throat. "Listen and continue to repeat as the words fall from my beak. Ahziz rurh, caliz duhr. Repeat it now, following me. Ahziz ruhr, caliz duhr."

Together they chanted it out. "Ahziz ruhr, caliz duhr!" They floated above the ground.

"The secret to flight is in these words. Antai yo, antai yo. Yee cohr rie, lisso mee. Yom!" They soared into the air.

"Yah hoo," yelled Dr. Sanders, as he swooped down to the tree tops carried by a gust of wind and rose again to rejoin his friends.

"John! Look what I can do!" yelled Ben's mom, as she spun like a ballerina with no effort at all.

Ben's dad turned over on his back, gliding as though he were on the open seas. Exuberantly, he said, "Who would ever believe me if I told them I could fly? I haven't been this happy since I was, I was six years old!" He spun back around so he could see the ground, nearly half a mile away.

The sight of a house that looked like a dot on the ground frightened him. His flight became irregular, and he started to lose altitude. "Eagle! Eagle! How do we get down?"

Eagle flew to his side, calmly reassuring him. "It's easy. Just wish it to be so. See yourself there down below. For any wish you have, in the sky or on the ground, can come true if you truly hear its sound."

Ben's dad shut his eyes. His flight steadied, and he stopped falling. Looking again, he surveyed the sky, but Eagle was nowhere to be found. It didn't matter. With a picture of the yard behind his house fixed firmly in his thoughts, he turned and shot to the earth, landing softly at the feet of Scrawlyknot.

Ben's mom and Dr. Sanders landed right behind him. When they touched the ground, gravity hardly tugged at their shoes. Inside, they felt as light as the softest down.

Eagle and Pere came to rest in the branches above Scrawlyknot's head. The great tree creature looked up. He could barely see them because of his bushy eyebrows. "Thank you, my friends. I am sure that what they have learned this day will repay us all, keeping doubters away." Returning his gaze to the gathering below, he raised his voice high. "Now that you have had a taste of the sky, let the festivities begin. Give a welcome, each of you, to the treemungermen."

The earth rumbled and shook. Trees shook the dirt. All around them large eyes peered out from the edge of the black soil.

"Come out, come out," coaxed Scrawlyknot. "Now is no time for hesitation. These people of Luan are your friends, too."

Everything moved and heaved. First the trees. The bushes followed. The flower creatures popped up their silly heads and laughed. Within moments, Dr. Sanders and Ben's parents were encircled by hundreds of treemungermen in all shapes and sizes. Together they sang in the sweetest voices. "Sing ho ho, sing ho ho, ah yee nah sen hah yah ho!" Some strummed their fingers against their trunks and others tapped their feet to keep time with the song's rhythm.

As they sang this melodious song over and over again, each treemungerman stepped forward, lightly placing one hand against Ben's cheek. Ben reached up and placed his hand over theirs for a moment, then released it.

All the while Ben's parents watched, amazed. His mother, caught up in all the excitement, thought she was holding her husband's hand, when in fact, she was holding the hand of a small treemungerman with a ligustrum bush growing out of his ears. And Ben's dad, as mesmerized as she, thought he was holding her hand, but was holding the hand of a treemungerchild who had a new oak sprouting from her forehead.

Ben's mom looked to her right as Ben's dad looked to his left. At the same instant they jumped back a step and broke loose of the handhold of these strange creatures. The treemungerman and the treemungerchild frowned, and their eyes drooped.

"I hurt your feelings. I'm so sorry," said Ben's mother. As her hand shook, she reached out to the treemungerman's closed hand, and touched it. With his eyes still to the ground, the treemungerman opened his hand and turned it palm up. She took it firmly. He looked up into her eyes, his frown turning to a smile. She embraced him.

"Will you forgive me?" asked Ben's dad as he took the hand of the treemungerchild. She looked up at him with a bright smile and offered her other hand. He took it and together they started to dance, slowly at first, then picking up speed. The rest of the treemungermen made a clearing for them, and hooped and hollered at the top of their mighty lungs.

"Sah yah bop bop woo!" screamed a big fellow with a juniper tree resting between his drooping ears.

"Sing a boo, sing a boo, col a la la lee!" sang two creatures arm and arm with two oaks that had grown together towering above their heads.

"Cree bee, cree bee, creeee beeee!" sang little treemungermen with tulips and daffodils dangling from their eyebrows.

"Sic co co, sic co co, yah too too happa happa ho!" sang a whole family of Sner-rocks with deep, hearty voices.

Faster and faster Ben's dad and the treemungerchild danced. Dr. Sanders slapped his thighs and, grabbing the hand of a treemungerman twice his size, jumped into the middle of the wild dance. His partner was swinging him around so fast that his feet left the ground, and his shoes went flying over the house and into the woods. When the treemungerman brought him down to earth again, Dr. Sanders was panting and gulping air. After he caught his breath, he said, "Let's do it again," and they were off for another round.

Scrawlyknot watched this wonderful celebration while clapping his large hands. Treemungermen, treemunger children, Sner-rocks, and all kinds of creatures, including the stream, shimmied and jumped until dust filled the air.

No one noticed as Ben sat and watched by himself. Even though this celebration was to honor him, the changes happening in his body made it hard to stand. To dance was painful, because small roots were actually pushing through the skin of his feet. All the same, he sang and wiggled his toes to the beat of the dancing giants.

Scrawlyknot bent over and stroked Ben's hair, then whispered into his ear. "Are you ready, child, to feel the earth's smile bubble through your feet?"

Ben warily nodded.

Scrawlyknot held his hand high. At first none of the treemungermen noticed his sign. But one by one they stopped where they were and turned to face him. The last to halt were the creatures dancing with Dr. Sanders and Ben's mom and dad. Shuffling to a full stop, they giggled nervously, self-consciously releasing their grip on their human friends. Dr. Sanders and Ben's parents looked about confused. They had all but forgotten where they were and the purpose of this momentous evening.

Scrawlyknot spoke slowly, choosing his words carefully. "My fellow treemungermen, and all new friends of the Kingdom of Nowt. Today is a new beginning. We have gathered to celebrate the re-rooting of the first Luanian since the age long, long ago. Ben has come to share his wisdom and courage, to give to that higher cause so that all of us might know life without flaws."

Scrawlyknot held one hand high in the air with his palm pointing to the heavens. With another hand he pointed with his woody finger to a bare spot on a grassy knoll. Then, a bolt of lightning came crashing through the upraised hand, and shot out his finger gouging a huge hole in the ground. It smoked from the burn of that great charge. Everyone in the circle jumped back. Many of the treemungermen fell to their knees, shaking. A thunderclap followed that seemed to rumble forever across the countryside. Ben's mom and dad fell into each other arms, and she hid her face in his chest.

Of all the treemungermen and human beings, Dr. Sanders stood his ground, not wavering an inch. Static electricity crackled in the air. His frizzy, grey hair stood on end. Standing beside him was Ben.

With his finger pointing directly at Ben, Scrawlyknot turned. "My friend, my dear Ben, now is the appointed hour to join us. What I do will hurt at first, but then the bubble will burst." Another large bolt of lightning cracked through the air and descended into Scrawlyknot's uplifted palm. It came whizzing out of his pointed finger right toward Ben. Instead of exploding, it wrapped him in a circle of light. Sparks threw off the colors of the rainbow in every direction. A warm glow engulfed him.

The stream snaked through the air like a serpent. As Ben reached out and touched it, the stream glowed like him. Scrawlyknot reached into the water and lit up as well. Following his lead, Dr. Sanders, Ben's parents, and each of the treemungermen did the same. They too were filled with a miraculous light.

Scrawlyknot boomed out, "May all gathered here never forget this night. For now we are bound together with the blood of light. Our fate carries us on to a destiny unknown. With faith we shall reach it by all that is now sown."

The water raised Ben up, carrying him high in the air. It retraced its winding path through all the creatures gathered in that grassy field until it hovered above the hole in the ground. Smoke still rose from the dirt. The stream poured itself into the earth and steam rose high into the air. Slowly, the water lowered Ben until his feet touched down.

Unexpectedly, a huge bolt of lightning shot straight from the sky to where Ben stood. It didn't just flash, but continued to connect him and the clouds which swirled above.

Everyone watched as Ben changed into something that looked more like a tree than a human being. The lightning disappeared. The smoke and steam cleared. Now, Ben stood no longer as a boy. He was like the Luanians of ages ago. His skin was rough like the bark of a tree. Small branches poked from his arms and the trunk of his body. And the roots, pushing through his feet, had already dug deep into the earth.

Tentatively, all the treemungermen, Scrawlyknot, Dr. Sanders, and Ben's parents inched forward to get a better view. He still had a face, but it now looked wizened and old. His clothes hung like tattered ribbons from his limbs. His skin had turned a grayish brown with moldy white spots peppering its surface. Ben moved his arm, but it creaked like a large tree limb blowing in the wind. Everyone crowded closer until they could touch him.

Dr. Sanders inched forward with a broad smile on his face. "Ah, my friends in the medical profession will have a tough time explaining this. A person who is also a tree. I love it. How are you feeling lad?"

"Okay, I think, Dr. Sanders."

"Good! That's what I wanted to hear. You've been through quite a lot this evening. It's my professional opinion that this young man, I mean, Luanian, needs some rest."

"I heartily agree," said Scrawlyknot. "When the world hears of his return, there will be no end to those who come to learn. Let's give the child room to breath for just this moment. He must prepare himself for the days ahead, for all those who truly wish to be fed." Scrawlyknot waved his hand.

At his command, all the treemungermen pulled back, leaving Ben with his mother, father, and Dr. Sanders at his side. One by one each treemungerman returned to the ground as the round globe of the sun peaked its early morning rays above the crown where Ben stood. All was quiet, for now.

Epilogue

The legend of Ben, Luanian and treemungerman, son of man and woman, spread across the land. Children and adults came daily to sit at his feet, and listen to his wise words. Scientists came to examine his strange physique, only to leave perplexed. The people of Luan turned away from destruction, and re-embraced the Kingdom of Nowt. And rarely a night went by when Luanians and treemungermen couldn't be seen dancing with Ben in the soft light of the moon.

The End

About the Author

Richard Stone is the author of *Stories: The Family Legacy*, a guide for sharing and recollection that has been used by hospice and healthcare professionals throughout the U.S. His newest book is *The Healing Art of Storytelling*. Articles and publications by or about Mr. Stone and his work have appeared in Utne Reader, Reader's Digest, Fortune Magazine, and Storytelling Magazine.

Richard is also the founder of the Storywork Institute, and has been a pioneer in the development of story-based training programs for healthcare organizations around the country, as well as team building, leadership development, and strategic planning programs for corporate clients such as Kaiser Permanente, Mayo Clinic, Walt Disney Imagineering, Kraft Foods, and Lucent Technologies.

Most recently, Richard founded the Imagine This Company, an organization that is developing television, educational curricula, and home based games and activities based on using storytelling as a tool to enhance the literacy and imaginative skills of children ages 8 to 15. Imagine This Company's first board game—Pitch-A-Story!—was just released and is available on the Web and at specialty retailers nationwide.

In addition, Richard has served as an adjunct professor at both the University of Central Florida and Valencia Community College teaching courses on storytelling and its applications in community life; developed the Disney Institute's StoryArts curricula; and, has taught and spoken throughout the world on the healing power of storytelling. He currently serves on the National Board of Directors of the International Storytelling Center in Jonesborough, TN.

Printed in the United States
39938LVS00001B/16-114

9 781420 874136